**"But just so you know, I don't mix business with pleasure."**

He hadn't asked her to.

She shot him a fiery look. "I may be a woman, but I can do my job."

"I never said you couldn't," Justin said.

"Good, I'm glad we got that out of the way."

He had to admit he was intrigued by her spunk. Obviously she'd battled her way up against men in her field who probably thought she was incompetent based on her sex.

Either that or they were sidetracked by her good looks.

He wouldn't make that mistake.

And he certainly couldn't or wouldn't allow her pretty little face to distract him. He was here to solve the case of the missing girls.

Nothing else mattered.

Especially the little zing of lightning that had sizzled between them when he'd brushed her hand earlier.

# COLD CASE AT CARLTON'S CANYON

---

## RITA HERRON

To my own hero, Lee—love you always,

Rita

ISBN-13: 978-0-373-74789-4

COLD CASE AT CARLTON'S CANYON

Copyright © 2014 by Rita B. Herron

Printed in U.S.A.

# ABOUT THE AUTHOR

Award-winning author Rita Herron wrote her first book when she was twelve, but didn't think real people grew up to be writers. Now she writes so she doesn't have to get a *real* job. A former kindergarten teacher and workshop leader, she traded storytelling to kids for writing romance, and now she writes romantic comedies and romantic suspense. She lives in Georgia with her own romance hero and three kids. She loves to hear from readers, so please write her at P.O. Box 921225, Norcross, GA 30092-1225, or visit her website, www.ritaherron.com.

## Books by Rita Herron

# CAST OF CHARACTERS

*Sheriff Amanda Blair*—She must accept help from Texas Ranger Justin Thorpe to solve a cold case involving a string of women's disappearances; only, she can't give her heart to the man.

*Sergeant Justin Thorpe*—He's in Sunset Mesa to solve a murder, not to get involved with the sexy sheriff. But when Amanda becomes a target, he will risk his life to protect her.

*Kelly Lambert*—Is her disappearance connected to the string of other missing women?

*Raymond Fisher*—Did he hurt Kelly because she'd decided to cancel the wedding?

*Terry Sumter*—Kelly's former boyfriend wanted her back; did he kill her because she turned him down?

*Renee Daly*—Did she kill Kelly to get her out of the way so she could have Raymond?

*Donald Reisling*—He was paralyzed in an accident ten years ago; does he have a grudge against the women who abandoned him after the accident?

*Mr. Reisling*—Has Donald's father been exacting revenge against the women himself the past ten years?

*Bernadette Willis*—She had emotional problems in high school and was also a target of bullying. Has she returned to the town for the high school reunion to make her former classmates pay?

*Ted Butts*—His brother Carlton committed suicide ten years ago because the popular teens bullied him. Has Ted been making women disappear out of revenge for his brother?

*Wynona Butts*—Carlton's mother was devastated over her son's death; does she have a vendetta against Amanda and the other women?

*Prologue*

Kelly Lambert did not want to die.

But the kind person who'd offered to give her a ride when her car broke down outside Sunset Mesa, the person she'd thought had saved her from walking late at night on a deserted road, had turned into a maniac.

A rancid breath bathed Kelly's cheek, and her stomach roiled.

"Please…" she begged.

Her words died as fingers tightened the belt around her throat. Rocks skittered beneath her feet as her attacker dragged her nearer the edge of the canyon and forced her to look at the rocky terrain below.

Hundreds of feet loomed between her and the ground. Even if she managed to land on the level part between the jagged rocks, the impact of the fall would kill her.

"That's where you belong," the crazed voice murmured. "Mean girls like you deserve to die."

"No, please stop," she gasped. "Why are you doing this to me?"

A pair of rage-filled eyes glittered back at her. "You know why."

Kelly's lungs strained for air as the leather dug into her throat.

But she didn't know. Didn't know why this person wanted her dead. Why anyone would want her dead.

Her attacker shoved her closer to the edge. Kelly's legs dangled over the canyon like a rag doll's.

She struggled again, desperate to escape, but whatever drug she'd been given had made her too weak. Fighting back was impossible. She couldn't move her hands, couldn't lift her arms, couldn't kick at all.

Tears streamed down her cheeks as the fingers dug deeper into her throat.

"No…"

Her attacker's bitter laugh echoed through the canyon, and Kelly gagged.

Her life flashed in front of her like a series of movie clips. Her mother braiding her hair before she'd died. Easter egg hunts, Christmases, proms and dance lessons.

High school boyfriends and college parties and… her upcoming wedding…

She had her dress picked out. The flowers…roses… the bridal shower she was supposed to have today.

And the honeymoon…a honeymoon she would never get to have.

Panic seized her, and pain knifed through her chest as the belt crushed her windpipe. Nausea mingled with terror and her head spun.

Then the lush green of spring faded into black as death came for her.

# Chapter One

Sergeant Justin Thorpe was a loner. Always had been. Always would be.

It was the very reason he was good at his job. No entanglements to tie him down or distract him.

He stared at the decomposed body of the girl floating in Camden Creek, trepidation knotting his gut.

He had a hunch this was one of the girls who'd disappeared from Sunset Mesa, although the medical examiner would have his work cut out to identify what was left of her. Other girls who'd gone missing from various counties across Texas were possibly connected, as well.

Too many girls.

At first no one had connected the disappearances, but Justin had noted that the women went missing in the spring, and that one fact had raised a red flag in his mind.

So far though he hadn't found any other connection. But he would. He just needed time.

Dr. Sagebrush, the ME who'd also worked a case

in Camden Creek involving a serious bus crash that had killed several teenagers a few years back, stooped down to study the body as two crime techs eased it onto the creek bank.

Thick trees shaded the area so the ME shone a flashlight over the corpse while crime techs searched the water and embankment with their own.

A tangled web of hair floated around the young woman's mud-streaked face, bones poked through the already decaying skin and there were bruises, scratches and teeth marks from animals that had picked at her marred body.

She was still clothed, her thin T-shirt torn and tattered, her jeans full of holes and layered in dirt.

The CSU team snapped pictures while Dr. Sagebrush adjusted his glasses and examined her.

"How long do you think she's been dead?" Justin asked.

"Hard to say yet," Dr. Sagebrush replied. "The temperature of the water could have slowed down decomp, but I'd guess a while. Maybe a couple of months."

Two young women had disappeared within that time frame.

Justin eyed the creek, scanning the terrain up and downstream with his flashlight. "You think she was dumped in the creek or floated in from the river?"

"Don't know." Dr. Sagebrush shrugged, his eyes narrowed as he pushed strands of wet hair away from the girl's face. "Look at this." The ME pointed to the bruises on her neck.

"She was strangled," Justin said, frowning at the angry, inch-wide red lines cutting into the woman's throat. "Looks like the killer used a belt."

Dr. Sagebrush nodded. "Probably the cause of death, but I can't say for sure till I get her on the table. If there's water in her lungs, she might have been alive when she was dumped."

Justin's stomach knotted as an image of the girl fighting for her last breath flashed in his eyes. The current in this part of the creek was strong, the rocks jagged. Kayakers and raft guides trained on the wider, rougher sections as practice for the river. If she was alive, she'd probably been too weak to fight the current and save herself.

But the doctor lifted the girl's eyelids, and Justin saw petechial hemorrhaging and guessed she'd died of strangulation.

One of the crime techs dragged a tennis shoe from the muddy bank, then compared it to the girl's foot. "Could have belonged to her. We'll bag it and see if we find anything on it."

Justin nodded. "I'll look around for forensics although, like you say, she probably wasn't killed here."

Justin knew the drill. He'd been working homicide cases, hunting serial killers and the most wanted, for ten years now. Nothing surprised him.

Yet a young woman's senseless murder still made sorrow fill his chest.

He walked over to the edge of the river and studied the foliage, then dipped deeper into the woods to search for any sign that the girl had lost her life nearby.

If they found hair or clothing, even a footprint, it might help track down the killer.

Anxiety twitched at his insides. Only two of the girls who'd gone missing in the past few years had been found. One dead; the other had run away.

But there was no sign of the others. No notes goodbye. No phone calls or ransom requests.

No bodies, making the police wonder if the girls were alive or dead.

So why had this woman's body been dumped where it could be found?

Were the cases connected? And if so, were any of the other young women still alive?

SHERIFF AMANDA BLAIR sipped her umpteenth cup of coffee for the day while she skimmed the mail on her desk. An envelope stamped with the high school's emblem and a sketch of the canyon for which the school had been named, Canyon High, caught her eye, and she ripped it open.

The invitation to her high school class reunion filled her with a mixture of dread and wariness.

She'd moved away from Sunset Mesa after her senior year when her father had been transferred.

Having grown up with a Texas Ranger for a father, she'd known she'd wanted to follow in his footsteps and work in law enforcement. And there had been nothing for her in Sunset Mesa. No best friend. No boyfriend.

No one who'd missed her or written her love letters or even asked what her plans were for the future.

Truthfully she'd been glad to move. She'd always been a loner, a tomboy, more interested in her father's cases than joining the girly girls at school with their silly obsessions with makeup, fashion and boys.

She'd chosen softball and the swim team over cheerleading and dance competitions and had felt more comfortable hanging out with guys at sports events than having sleepovers or going shopping with her female peers.

The one event that had colored her entire high school experience was her classmate Carlton Butts's death.

Juniors in high school were not supposed to die. They especially weren't supposed to commit suicide.

Regret, that she hadn't been a better friend to him and sensed how deep his depression ran, taunted her. She'd had nightmares about him plunging to the bottom of the canyon for years. In fact, most people in town now referred to the canyon as Carlton's Canyon—some even called the high school Carlton Canyon High.

Occasionally she even thought she heard Carlton whispering her voice in the night. Calling to her for help.

Begging her to save him from himself.

Only she'd missed the signs.

Guilt had driven her to search for answers, only none had ever come. Then young women had started disappearing across Texas, two from Sunset Mesa, and she'd felt her heart tugging at her to return to the town. To find out what was happening to them because she'd failed to help her own friend.

When the deputy position had come available in Sunset Mesa, she'd requested it. Sheriff Lager had been a friend of her father's and had handpicked her for the job.

Then she'd realized that he was suffering from dementia. He eventually admitted he knew he had issues and told her his plans to retire.

Sighing, she stuffed the invitation to the reunion back in the envelope, doubting that she would attend. There was no one from her class she particularly wanted to see.

But what if one of them knew something about one of the missing women? It was her job to find the answers.

What better way to get the scoop than at an informal gathering where everyone was supposed to be friends?

Intrigued by the idea, she tucked the invitation into the calendar on her desk, then added the date to her phone calendar. Plans that week included a family picnic on Friday, then a cocktail party and dance on Saturday night.

No family or husband for her.

Memories of watching Julie Kane and Thurston Howard sharing the prom king and queen dance drifted back, reminding her how much of a wallflower she'd been.

*You're not an eighteen-year-old geeky kid anymore, Amanda. You're sheriff.*

And a stupid high school reunion was not going to turn her back into the shy awkward girl she'd once been.

The door to the front of the sheriff's office suddenly burst open, and Amanda looked up.

Larry Lambert, the manager at the local bank, rushed in, his normally friendly face strained with worry. A younger man, probably in his late twenties, stood beside him, his hair spiked as if he'd run his hands through it a dozen times. Tension vibrated between the men, a chill in the air.

Amanda stepped from behind her desk. "Mr. Lambert—"

"You have to help us, Sheriff Blair," Mr. Lambert said. "My daughter Kelly…" The six-foot-tall man broke down, tears streaming from his eyes. "She didn't come home last night."

Amanda's heart clenched. Spring was supposed to be a time of renewed life. Instead, a woman had gone missing just as one had every spring the past few years. A woman she'd gone to high school with. A woman close to her own age.

Which broke the pattern. Kelly was older than the teens who'd disappeared.

Still, could she have met foul play?

Was Kelly dead or could she still be alive?

JUSTIN WAS ANXIOUS for the results of the autopsy and crime scene findings, but his early-morning phone call had gone unanswered. Suspicious that the girl was one of the missing ones from Sunset Mesa, he decided to visit the sheriff and give her a heads-up.

He'd spoken to her after Sheriff Camden from Camden Crossing had conferred with her about the disappearance of his own sister and Peyton Boulder, two girls who'd disappeared after a fatal bus crash seven years ago. At first they'd thought the cold case might be related to the string of missing persons from Sunset Mesa, but they'd discovered it wasn't.

Dry farmland and terrain passed by him as he veered onto the highway toward Sunset Mesa. He'd heard that the town had gotten its name because of the beautiful colors of the sunset.

Radiant oranges, reds and yellows streaked the sky, painting a rainbow effect over the canyon that was so beautiful it made him wish he was here on vacation, not hunting down a killer. But he never stayed in one place more than a few days and wouldn't get attached to this town either.

He navigated the road leading into Sunset Mesa, wondering about the new sheriff in town.

He'd met her once and she seemed okay, but he hoped to hell she wasn't some flake, that she had a head on her shoulders and would cooperate with him. Police work was his life, and he couldn't tolerate a law officer who wasn't committed to the job.

A small ranch pointed to the north; then the sign for Sunset Mesa popped into view. Like every other small town he'd been in, the town was built on a square. The buildings looked aged, a Western flair to the outsides, a park in the middle of town with small local businesses surrounding it.

The sheriff's office/jail/courthouse was housed at the far right, an adobe structure painted the same orange that he'd noted in the sunset.

Early-evening shadows flickered along the pavement as he parked in front of the building, climbed out, adjusted his Stetson and strode to the front door. When he'd first spoken to Sheriff Blair, he'd formed an image of her in his mind.

Her voice had held a husky note, a sign she was probably mannish. Then he'd met her briefly once and realized she was nothing like he'd pictured.

Even the sheriff's uniform hadn't disguised her curves and beauty. Not that it mattered what she looked like. He was here to do a job and nothing else.

The dead girl's face taunted him, and he straightened and opened the door. Getting justice for that victim was his priority.

Once he'd failed at his job and it had cost another young girl her life. He wouldn't fail this time.

No one would stop him from finding answers.

Wood floors creaked with his boots as he entered, the pale yellow walls and artwork reminiscent of days gone by. A row of black and white photographs of the town and the canyon lined one wall, rugged landscapes on another.

A noise echoed from the back and he frowned. Heated voices. A man's.

No, two men's.

He rapped on the wall by the door leading to the back. A minute later, a woman appeared wearing the sheriff's uniform.

A petite woman with lush curves and hair the reddish-brown color of autumn leaves. Amanda Blair. Rather—Sheriff Amanda Blair.

Her looks sucker punched him again.

Eyes the color of a copper penny stared up at him, a strained look on her pretty face.

"Hello, ma'am." He tipped his Stetson. "I don't know if you remember me, but I'm Sergeant Justin Thorpe with the Texas Rangers."

She looked him up and down, and for the first time in his life, he wondered if he came up lacking. Not that he usually cared about a coworker's opinion of him, but something about her made him want her admiration.

But her look gave nothing away. "Yes, I remember."

He couldn't tell from her tone how she meant the comment. But it didn't sound good.

"Did someone call you about coming here today?"

He frowned, confused. Maybe she'd already heard about the body they found. "No, I needed to talk to you about the missing-persons cases."

"You heard about Kelly Lambert?"

"Kelly Lambert?" Justin tried to remember the names of all the women on the list so far, but hers didn't ring a bell. Had she received word about the identification of the body before he did?

Her expression clouded. "The girl who just disappeared last night. Her father and fiancé are in my office now."

Justin's gut clenched. That explained the raised voices. But Kelly Lambert wasn't the woman they'd found in the creek because that woman had been there for months.

Which meant Kelly Lambert might still be alive.

Dammit, he and Sheriff Blair needed to find her before she ended up dead like the poor woman they'd just dragged from the water.

## Chapter Two

Amanda fought the fluttering of awareness that rippled through her at the sight of the tall, dark handsome Texas Ranger. She'd met him briefly once when Sheriff Camden from Camden Crossing had asked them to confer on the case involving his sister, and had finally managed to get his sexy image out of her head.

Now he was here. Back. Planning to work with her.

And dammit, she needed his help.

She couldn't help but stare at him. He towered over her, his massive shoulders stretching taut against his Western shirt, his green eyes a surprise with his dark coloring and black hair.

She sized up his other features—a chiseled jaw, a crooked nose that had probably been broken and a cleft in his chin. By themselves his features didn't stand out, but the combination made him look tough, rugged, a man not to be messed with.

But that silver star of Texas shining on his shirt reminded her that he was here on business.

Amanda never mixed business with pleasure.

She'd worked too hard to overcome the stigma of being a female in a man's world and couldn't backtrack by getting involved with a coworker.

No one would respect her then.

"I think we'd better start over," Sgt. Thorpe said. "You said that another woman has gone missing?"

Amanda nodded. "Kelly Lambert. She didn't make it home last night and her father and fiancé haven't heard from her."

"So it's been less than twenty-four hours," Justin said. "Too early to file a report."

Amanda shrugged. "Actually it has been over twenty-four hours. They haven't heard from her since early yesterday morning. She's been planning her wedding, and she never made it to her bridal shower this afternoon. A shower she was supposedly excited about."

"Maybe she got cold feet and ran off."

"It's possible, but I didn't get the impression that she was that kind of girl from her father and the groom-to-be." Amanda folded her arms. "Wait a minute. If you didn't know about Kelly, why are you here?"

The Ranger's mouth twitched. "Because the body of a young woman was discovered in Camden Creek earlier."

Amanda's chest started to ache. "You think it's Kelly?"

Suddenly a choked sound echoed from behind her,

and Amanda spun around to see Mr. Lambert and Kelly's fiancé standing at the doorway.

"You found her?" Mr. Lambert asked in a broken voice.

Kelly's fiancé, Raymond Fisher, paled. "Please, God, no…"

Amanda tensed and glanced at Sergeant Thorpe. "Mr. Lambert, Mr. Fisher, this is Sergeant Thorpe with the Texas Rangers. Sergeant Thorpe?"

Justin motioned with his hands as if to calm the panic in the men's eyes. "We haven't identified the young woman yet, but it's not Kelly. The ME thinks this woman has been dead a couple of months."

Relief mingled with horror on the father's face. "But you think this woman's death is related to Kelly's disappearance?"

The fiancé stumbled forward and sank into a wooden chair near the desk. He leaned his head on his hands, a sob escaping. "You think she's dead, don't you?"

Amanda's mind raced to the missing-persons file on her desk. Carly Edgewater and Tina Grimes were recent names on the list. It could be one of them.

But compassion for the fiancé and Kelly's father forced her to keep her thoughts to herself. She was a professional. Her job was to find answers.

She also needed to keep these men calm. If Kelly had been abducted, they might know something to help track down the kidnapper.

"It's too early to tell that," Amanda said as she

patted Fisher's shoulder. "Right now all we know is that Kelly didn't show up for her bridal shower and hasn't contacted you. Maybe Sergeant Thorpe is right and Kelly just needed some time alone. She could have ducked out to think things over before the wedding."

"No," Fisher said with a firm shake of his head. "Kelly wouldn't run out on me. She loved me, and I loved her. She was excited about the wedding."

"He's right," Lambert said. "Kelly wasn't the kind of girl to run out on anyone. She was dependable, smart, had a good head on her shoulders." He fumbled with his phone and angled it toward Amanda. "Even if she did want some time, she would have told one of us. I've called her at least fifty times in the last few hours, and she hasn't answered or returned my calls."

"I've called her, too," Fisher said, pulling out his phone. "I've sent dozens of texts, too, but she hasn't responded. I even drove by her place, but her car wasn't there and neither was she."

"What kind of car does she drive?" Amanda asked.

"A red Toyota."

"Do you know the license plate?"

He jotted it on a sticky note from her desk.

Sergeant Thorpe exhaled. "I understand your concern," he said in a gruff voice. "Sheriff Blair and I will do everything we can to find your daughter."

Amanda's lungs squeezed for air as she stepped

aside to call her deputy, Joe Morgan. She quickly explained the situation.

"Drive around and see if you can find Kelly's car. She drives a red Toyota." She gave him the license plate and hung up. Maybe if they located Kelly's car, they'd find a clue as to what had happened to her.

She just hoped they found her alive.

JUSTIN CONSIDERED THE circumstances and knew he had to remain objective and treat this woman's disappearance like he would any other case. To assume Kelly had been abducted by the same person who'd killed the woman in the creek—and possibly a half dozen others who still hadn't been located—was too presumptuous.

Making assumptions was dangerous. It could lead him to miss important details and send him on a wild goose chase.

After all, it was possible that Kelly's fiancé was lying. He and Kelly could have had a major blow-up and she could have run off. She might need time to compose herself before contacting her father. Or hell, she might be off planning some sort of surprise for her fiancé.

But his gut instincts told him they were dealing with a serial criminal who'd been kidnapping female victims for nearly a decade and would continue until he was stopped.

But he wouldn't be doing his job if he didn't explore every option. With the publicity surrounding the ongoing missing-persons case, someone could use the disappearances as a smoke screen to cover up a more personal murder.

Like a fiancé getting rid of his girlfriend if she decided to call off the wedding...

"Sheriff, why don't you take Mr. Lambert back for coffee while I talk to Mr. Fisher for a few minutes?"

Amanda's gaze met his, questions looming, but separating victims or suspects was customary, so she nodded.

"Come on, Mr. Lambert. I'll start the paperwork for the missing-persons report." She glanced at Justin and Fisher. "Would you guys like coffee?"

Fisher shook his head no. "I don't think my stomach could handle it right now."

"Coffee would be good," Justin said. "Black."

Her brows rose a second as if to say that she wasn't his maid, and his mouth quirked. After all, she had offered.

She led Lambert back through the door to the back and returned a moment later with a bottle of water for Fisher and a cup of coffee for him.

"Thanks," he said with a small smile.

A zing of something like attraction hit him when her hand brushed his as she gave him the mug. Her mouth twisted into a frown as if she'd noticed it, too, and she jerked her hand away and rushed back to talk to Lambert.

Sweat trickled down Fisher's forehead. Was he

simply upset about Kelly's disappearance or was he nervous because he was hiding something?

Justin took a sip of coffee, surprised at the taste. Most law enforcement workers could handle a gun but didn't know a flying fig about how to brew decent coffee.

Amanda Blair could do both. Intriguing.

"Mr. Fisher, how long have you and Kelly been together?" Justin asked.

Fisher gripped the water bottle with white-knuckled hands. "We knew each other in high school but didn't date until our senior year. We got engaged last Christmas. Kelly took some time after high school to do some mission trips, then decided to get her teaching degree. She just graduated with a masters in education and is looking for a teaching job."

"What do you do?"

Fisher shrugged. "I'm a financial consultant. I just started with a new company in Austin. We were moving there after the wedding."

"Any problems between you and Kelly lately?"

Fisher shook his head, his leg bouncing up and down. "No."

"No recent fights? Arguments over where you'd live? Money?"

"Not really. We get along great."

"Do you and Kelly live together?"

Fisher nodded. "We moved in together our senior year of college."

"What did her father think about that?"

"At first he wasn't too happy," Fisher admitted. "But eventually he realized it made sense. And when a student was raped on campus, he said he was actually relieved she was living with me." Emotions made his voice warble. "He felt like she was…safe."

Justin heard the guilt in Fisher's tone. He understood that kind of guilt. "Do Kelly and her father get along?"

Fisher frowned up at him. "Yeah, why?"

"Anything you tell us about Kelly might help us find her," Justin hedged. "So they get along?"

Fisher nodded. "Kelly's mother died a while back and they went through a rough patch. That was before we started dating. But they were both grieving and adjusting. She said the last two years they've been close."

"How did her mother die?"

"Cancer. She was sick a long time."

So no skeletons that might suggest Lambert had hurt her. "What did Mr. Lambert think about the upcoming marriage?"

Fisher sipped his water again. "He was cool with it."

"But?"

Fisher shifted in the seat. "At first he wanted her to wait until we saved more money. But Kelly assured him we'd be okay."

"You have money?" Justin asked.

Fisher shrugged. "A little. I had scholarships for

college, so I saved over the summers, enough to get us by until we both started getting paid."

"So Mr. Lambert gave you his approval?"

"Yes," Fisher said a little curtly. "Now why all these questions? Shouldn't you be doing something to find Kelly?"

"We will do everything possible, Mr. Fisher. But like I said earlier, we need to know everything about Kelly to help us." He hesitated and decided to take another tactic. "You said Lambert wanted you to wait until you were more financially sound. Did he offer to help out financially?"

Fisher shook his head. "He was paying for the wedding, but not our rent or bills. I saved the money for a down payment on a house."

Admirable of the young man. Maybe he had nothing to do with Kelly's disappearance.

If not, he'd have to look at the father.

And the serial killer they had nothing on yet…

"How are Lambert's finances?" Justin asked.

"He owns the bank in town. How do you think?"

"Being a smart ass won't help you," Justin said, his voice sharp with warning.

The young man shoved his hands through his hair. "Sorry, I'm just nervous and worried." He gripped the edges of the seat. "I feel like I need to be out looking for Kelly."

He'd check Lambert's financials just to verify Fisher's statement. If Lambert needed money and had an insurance policy on his daughter, that would provide motive. Although, the man appeared visibly distraught.

If he had money and had nothing to do with her disappearance, and this case wasn't related to the serial kidnapper, Lambert might receive a ransom call.

Fisher unscrewed the lid of the water bottle and swallowed a huge gulp.

"What about arguments between the two of you?"

A slight hesitation. "We disagreed over seating my uncle Jim next to her cousin Monique 'cause Monique will talk your head off. But that was small stuff. Nothing she'd leave me over."

"How about exes?"

His lips tightened, and he glanced to the doorway. "Her old boyfriend, Terry, called her a couple of weeks ago. Said he heard she was getting married and wanted to talk to her before we tied the knot."

"Talk to her about what?" Justin asked.

Fisher shrugged, dropped the water bottle cap, then bent over and picked it up.

"She didn't tell you?" Justin pushed.

"No," Fisher said. "I asked her if she still had feelings for him, but she laughed it off."

"Did *he* still have feelings for her?"

Fisher toyed with the bottle cap, rolling it between his fingers. "She said he didn't."

"But?"

Fisher scowled. "But I saw a text he sent her and it sure as hell sounded like he did."

The anger in the man's tone raised Justin's suspicions. "Did she agree to see him?"

Fisher squeezed his eyes shut for a moment, then opened them and took another sip of water. "I don't know. When she didn't come last night, I thought... maybe she'd met up with him."

Justin pushed a pad in front of Fisher. "I'll need his name and any information you have on him."

"I don't know his number, but his name is Terry Sumter."

"When was the last time you saw or spoke with Kelly?" Justin asked.

Kelly's fiancé dropped his head into his hands with a pained sigh. "Yesterday morning for breakfast," Fisher said. "We had waffles, then she said she had a million things to do—a dress fitting, shopping for bridesmaids' gifts.... The list went on and on." Regret flickered in his eyes. "I was only half listening. I had no idea it might be the last time I ever saw her."

Justin gritted his teeth. The man's fear sounded sincere. So did his guilt.

But were his guilt and fear real because he was afraid of getting caught?

"She was supposed to come home last night?"

He nodded, rubbing at his eyes. "I called and called and finally I received a text saying she was going to spend the night with one of her girlfriends."

"Which one?"

"Betty Jacobs," he said. "But when I called Kelly

this morning and she didn't answer, I tried Betty and she said Kelly hadn't been there."

Justin would pull everything he could find on the ex-boyfriend as well as Kelly's phone records and Fisher's.

Three different scenarios skittered through his head.

Kelly could have met with the old boyfriend, decided she'd made a mistake in agreeing to marry Fisher and run off with him.

Or Sumter could have tried to convince her to leave with him and either kidnapped or killed her when she'd refused.

Or Fisher could have discovered Kelly had feelings for her ex, and fought with her about it and killed her…either accidentally or in a fit of rage.

THE PHOTOGRAPH OF Kelly Lambert went up on the wall beside the other girls'.

All such pretty young women with their glossy hair, perfect lips and orthodontist-enhanced smiles.

All girls who were ugly on the inside and deserved to die.

One by one they would leave this world.

And everyone at Canyon High would know the reason why.

## Chapter Three

Amanda knew dividing Lambert from Fisher was the best police approach. If one of them was lying or hiding something, separating them was the best way to get the truth. But she didn't intend to let the Texas Ranger run her investigation or tell her what to do.

Lambert glanced back at the door, a nervous twitch to his eye. "What's that Ranger talking to Raymond about?"

"Just asking routine questions, finding out background information," Amanda said. "It helps us to get a full picture of Kelly. He'll want to know who her girlfriends are, when Raymond last saw her, anything that might help us figure out what happened to her."

"We have to find her," Lambert said. "I lost my wife… I can't lose Kelly. She's everything to me."

Sympathy for the man made Amanda squeeze his shoulder. "I promise you, Mr. Lambert, that Sergeant Thorpe and I will do everything we can to find Kelly and bring her back home to you."

He glanced down and studied his knuckles.

Amanda narrowed her eyes. He had scrapes on his left hand. A gash on his right.

She casually poured them both coffee, an image of Kelly at eighteen, when she'd won an award for most congenial, flitting through her head. "What happened to your hands?" she asked, sliding a cup of coffee in front of him.

He twisted his fingers in front of him, his expression odd as if he didn't remember. "I...was nervous when Kelly didn't call me back. Went outside and cut some wood. Guess I scraped my knuckles."

His explanation was feasible. Still...his daughter was missing.

"We'll need a current photograph of Kelly for the media and to spread around to other law enforcement agencies."

Lambert reached inside his back pocket, removed his wallet and pulled out a picture of her. Amanda's heart tugged. Kelly had always been pretty and had grown more so. She was dressed in a print dress, her long hair sweeping her shoulders.

"That was a couple of months ago," Lambert said. "I took her to the club to discuss the wedding plans."

Amanda studied the photo, thinking of her own father and how special their father/daughter dates had been.

Worry gnawed at her for Kelly's sake.

If Kelly had been kidnapped by the same person who'd abducted the other girls, they might never find her.

Kelly could already be dead.

Or…she could be suffering now.

Which meant every minute counted.

Amanda claimed the chair across from Lambert. "You say your daughter was excited about the wedding. Does she have any enemies that you know of?"

Another wave of sadness washed over the man's face. "No. Everyone loves her. In high school she was voted most congenial and most likely to succeed."

Amanda had forgotten about the most-likely-to-succeed award.

"In college, she worked on the school newspaper," her father continued, "then earned her degree in English and planned to teach high school. She's been applying for jobs and hopes to start in the fall."

Amanda cradled her own coffee cup, aiming for a casual tone. "You and Kelly get along?"

"Oh, yes," he said. "Kelly means everything to me." He coughed. "When we lost her mother, she was depressed, and at first I thought what the hell am I going to do with a teenage girl? But then…we both missed Janelle and…" His eyes flooded with tears as he looked up at her. "She's a good girl, Sheriff. A good girl."

"I know she is," Amanda said, battling to keep her compassion at bay so she could ask the tough questions that needed to be asked. The first rule of police work was not to let your emotions get involved. Her father had taught her that, God rest his soul.

"How about her and Raymond?" she asked. "Do they have any problems?"

"Not that I know of," Lambert said. "She adores him. I wanted them to take it slower, not marry till they had more money in the bank, but they insisted on going ahead, said they'd survive on love."

Amanda grimaced. She'd never been that naive. Maybe because she didn't believe in love. Her mother and father sure as hell hadn't loved each other.

"Mr. Lambert, what about you? Do *you* have any enemies?"

His eyes widened. "You think this might be about me?"

"I don't know, but we have to look at all the possibilities."

He stood and paced across the room. "No, I mean I own the bank and a few people got angry at me because I turned down loans. Filed a couple of foreclosures. But that's business."

Money was a powerful motivator. "I'll need their names."

He paused in his pacing, smoothing his hands down his suit jacket. "All right."

"Tell me about your financial situation," she said. "Do you have a large portfolio of investments? A big savings account?"

"You mean in case we receive a ransom call?"

"Yes," Amanda said. "That's a possibility." In fact, it would be preferable to the alternative. If someone called with a ransom request, they might have a chance of saving Kelly and catching the kidnapper.

"I have some money," he admitted. "Enough."

"Enough that someone might take your daughter to force you to pay them off?"

He paled. "If this is about money, I'll pay whatever they ask."

"Just make me a list of all of the people who might have a grievance against you," Amanda said. "We'll also need a list of all of Kelly's friends so we can talk to them."

"Of course."

He headed back to the chair but paused by the whiteboard in the corner. Amanda tensed. On the back of that board she'd tacked photos of all the missing women from the past ten years. She didn't want him to see them. "Mr. Lambert, sit down and—"

But a strangled sound escaped Lambert as he flipped it over. He staggered back, shaking his head in denial.

Anger hardened his voice when he spoke. "You haven't found any of those girls, have you? And you're not going to find my Kelly either."

Fear mingled with anger in Amanda's chest. She'd inherited the ongoing case from Sheriff Lager, but Kelly had gone missing on her watch. An image of the pretty woman's face taunted her. Kelly was her age, vibrant, planning her wedding. Looking forward to having a family and a long life ahead of her.

But her life might already have been cut off because some crazy maniac had targeted her.

And Amanda didn't have a clue as to who it was.

What if Lambert was right? What if she couldn't save Kelly in time?

JUSTIN TAPPED THE notepad in front of Fisher. "Make a list of the groomsmen in the wedding and their contact information for me."

Anger blazed in Fisher's eyes as he realized the implication. "What the hell? Kelly's father and I came here for help, and now you're treating me like a suspect. You think I had something to do with Kelly's disappearance?"

Justin forced his voice to remain level. The majority of missing-persons cases wound back to the family members or close friends. The fact that a string of females around the same age had gone missing was suspicious, but he couldn't discount anything at this point.

"I didn't say that. But it's important for us to talk to everyone who knew Kelly," Justin said. "Female and male friends included. Maybe one of them saw or heard something that could be helpful."

Fisher shot up, glaring at Justin. "That's bull. You want to ask them how Kelly and I got along. If I was jealous enough of an old boyfriend to hurt her."

"I will ask that, but it's routine," Justin said. "The first thing we do in an investigation is to clear family members and friends. Oftentimes, someone may tell us some detail to help us—it might be something small that you don't even think is important."

He motioned to the chair. "Now, if you want us to find Kelly, sit down and make that list. You're wasting valuable time."

Fisher's gaze met his, his eyes stormy with emotions and red rimmed from crying or lack of sleep. Maybe both.

Finally he released a heavy sigh and dropped back into the chair. "All right. But I love Kelly, and I'd never do anything to hurt her."

Justin studied him, wondering how he'd react if he was in this man's shoes. He'd be tearing apart the office, demanding answers, pushing for the police to comb the streets.

Ready to kill the person who'd stolen his fiancé.

That is, if that was what had happened.

Fisher took the pen and began to scribble names and phone numbers.

Sheriff Blair and Lambert appeared in the doorway, Lambert's face ashen.

"Mr. Lambert, Mr. Fisher, I'd like your permission to put a trace on your phones," Sheriff Blair said. "Just in case Kelly calls, or you receive a ransom call. We'll also need to look at Kelly's computer and phone records."

"Of course, whatever you need," Fisher said.

"Yes, check the phone records and computer." Lambert's eyes cut toward her. "Do whatever you have to do. Just find my daughter."

Sheriff Blair nodded, but she looked worried. "I'll get Kelly's picture in the missing-persons database and on the news right away. Hopefully someone saw something and we'll get a lead."

Fisher shoved the paper into Justin's hands. "Call us if you find her."

Fisher huffed, then strode out the door. Lambert glanced at Justin. "I saw the pictures of those other young women back there. I don't want Kelly's picture up there. I want you to find this bastard."

Justin shook the man's hand. "Yes, sir. We'll do everything we can."

"Do more than that," Lambert said sharply. Heaving a labored breath, he followed Fisher out the door.

Justin couldn't blame the man for being angry and frustrated. He didn't even know Kelly Lambert, and he felt like kicking something.

"I didn't mean for him to see the wall of photos," Sheriff Blair said.

"He's scared," Justin said. "Do you believe him?"

Sheriff Blair winced and gestured toward the notepad in her hand. "I think he loves her. I want to look at his financials. He turned down some folks for loans this year, had to foreclose on a couple of people."

Justin arched a brow. "So this could be about money?"

"We'll see if he receives a ransom call," Sheriff Blair said. "Maybe someone he angered decided to get their loan money from him after all."

"Revenge is a powerful motivator," Justin agreed.

"What about the fiancé?" she asked.

"He seems sincerely distraught, but it could be an act. Apparently a former boyfriend contacted Kelly recently and wanted to see her before the wedding. He or Fisher could have had a jealous streak."

Sheriff Blair nodded. "I'll have my deputy pull financials and talk to the folks at the bank." She made the call while he finished his coffee.

"I have a list of Fisher's friends and the ex's name and phone number," he said as she turned back to him. "I'll request Kelly's phone records and access to her computer as well as Fisher's and the ex's."

"Sounds like a plan," Sheriff Blair said. "At least a beginning."

"Maybe we'll find something at Kelly's place."

"Let's go," Sheriff Blair said. "You can make the phone calls in the car."

Justin followed her outside, then climbed in the passenger seat as he removed his phone from the clip on his belt. "Sheriff, if we're going to work together on this case, let's start by getting on a first-name basis."

An almost panicked look flickered in her eyes, making him wonder why she was so wary. Was it him personally or his badge that she didn't like?

"All right," she said tightly. "But just so you know, I don't mix business with pleasure."

He hadn't asked her to.

She shot him a fiery look. "I may be a woman, but I can do my job."

"I never said you couldn't," Justin said. Although her statement told him far more about her and her past than she probably realized.

Amanda chewed her bottom lip as she started the engine. "Good, I'm glad we got that out of the way."

He had to admit he was intrigued at her spunk. Obviously she'd battled her way up against men in her field who probably thought she was incompetent based on her sex.

Either that or they were sidetracked by her good looks.

He wouldn't make that mistake.

And he certainly couldn't or *wouldn't* allow her pretty little face to distract him. He was here to find Kelly Lambert and to solve the case of the missing girls.

Nothing else mattered.

Especially the little zing of lightning that had sizzled between them when he'd brushed her hand earlier.

THE DATES FOR the tenth reunion had been posted on the marquis in front of the high school. The members of that graduating class were returning to town to celebrate their accomplishments.

They would be partying and drinking and rehashing their fun times. The pep rallies. The football game wins. The dances. The bonfires by the canyon.

Graduation night.

They'd all be happy and laughing, bragging about their accomplishments and careers and awards. Showing off their wives and husbands, and their children.

Back together for the first time in years.

Which would make it easier to find the next ones who had to die.

## Chapter Four

Amanda silently chided herself. She shouldn't have blurted out that comment about being able to do her job.

But Sergeant Thorpe's—*Justin's*—suggestion that they use first names felt somehow intimate. Friendly.

Tempting.

Because he was the first man she'd met in years that made her want to forget her vow to not get involved with a coworker.

But doing so would mean losing his respect.

And holding on to her respect was all she had. She'd had her heart broken too many times to trust it to someone again.

Her own mother had left her father because she'd said he was married to the job.

Amanda was like her father—married to the job, too.

Justin phoned his superior to request phone records for Kelly, her father, her fiancé and her ex-boyfriend, then disconnected.

"Your father was a Texas Ranger, wasn't he?"

His question took her by surprise. "How did you know?" Had he researched her?

"I saw his photo on the wall at the central office. He was a hero."

She focused back on the road to keep her emotions at bay. He'd been gone for five years, but his death had left a hole in her heart. "Yeah, he was."

"He died saving a little boy?"

She nodded, proud of her dad. Yet his death had left her alone.

Still, she had to understand his devotion. She was just as dedicated to the job as he had been. In fact, she'd always wanted to be just like him.

But she didn't want to talk about personal things, especially her own life, with Justin. So she remained silent as she turned onto the highway leading to Kelly Lambert's apartment.

She parked in front of the complex and searched the numbers. Then she and Justin walked up to the door together. Fisher had already arrived, and he let them in, his expression guarded.

"I don't know what you think you'll find here," he said. "But go ahead and look around."

Amanda noticed boxes stacked everywhere. "You were moving?"

Fisher nodded. "We bought a house near my new job. The movers were supposed to come tomorrow." His voice cracked. "We wanted to get moved in before the wedding. I was supposed to start work the day after we returned from the honeymoon."

He ran his hand over one of the unclosed boxes, which held kitchenware, looking lost for a moment as if he didn't know what to do.

Justin cleared his throat. "Where's Kelly's computer?"

Fisher gestured toward an oak desk in the corner, and Justin addressed Amanda. "I'll take a look at it if you want to search the place."

She agreed and started in the kitchen while he slid onto the desk chair and booted up Kelly's laptop.

Fisher paced for a minute, then seemed startled when his phone jangled. "It's my new boss," he said before stepping onto the back patio to take the call.

Amanda opened kitchen cabinet doors, noting they were empty, then checked the drawers. Kelly must have already packed up all the silverware and kitchen supplies. She scanned the counters, finding a bottle opener and a basket with a couple of envelopes inside.

A power bill and a bank statement. She pulled out the statement and skimmed the summary of transactions. The grocery store, household bills, a payment to the florist and wedding caterer made two days before, all signs Kelly had planned to go through with the wedding.

Her account still held five thousand dollars, not enough money to warrant anyone kidnapping her for it. Then again, Kelly's father was the one with the big bucks.

Satisfied the kitchen held no answers, she headed

toward the couple's bedroom, but the refrigerator caught her eye. A magnet held Kelly's wedding invitation. Beside it, she noticed the invitation to the high school reunion.

The reunion was the week before Kelly's wedding. The timing meant that a lot of Kelly's friends would be in town. That is, if she still kept up with them.

Unlike her, Kelly had been a popular girl.

Moving on, she stepped into the bedroom. An eight-by-ten of Kelly and Fisher sat atop the dresser, the couple embracing for a romantic kiss. Both looked completely happy and in love.

More boxes were stacked on the floor. Most of the dresser drawers were empty, but when she opened the closet door, she found a long white satin wedding gown hanging inside. Pearl buttons ran down the back to the waist, where the gown flared with yards of organza and lace.

It was a beautiful dress; Kelly would have been a beautiful bride.

Had her life been cut short?

So far, her fiancé and father's stories held up. She wanted to talk to Kelly's girlfriends next. They might be able to shed some light on whether or not Fisher or Kelly's father should be considered suspects.

If they were innocent, she couldn't afford to waste too much time on them. Every minute she did meant whoever had taken Kelly was getting away.

If the same person who'd abducted the other missing girls had abducted Kelly, what was the reason? How was he choosing his victims?

Studying victimology could help her find answers.

Her cell phone buzzed, and she saw it was her deputy, Joe Morgan, so she snatched it up. "Hey, Joe, what's up?"

"I got your message and will look into the bank angle. But I found Kelly Lambert's car."

"Where?"

"Off of Old River Mill Road."

Amanda held her breath. "Was Kelly in it?"

"No," Deputy Morgan said. "The car had nosedived into a ditch. There are skid marks on the road as if another car ran her off the road."

Possibly a hit and run? "I'll call a crime unit to lift the tire prints."

"I'll wait here for them. By the way, Kelly's car is red, but I noticed pewter gray paint on the side. I'll have them take samples of the paint, too."

"Good work, Deputy. Did you search the area for Kelly? Maybe it was a hit and run and she's lying hurt nearby?"

"I already looked. She's not here, Sheriff. But I found a blood trail leading from Kelly's car to the edge of the road."

Amanda's lungs constricted. So Kelly was hurt.

If the driver had forced Kelly to go with him, where was she now?

JUSTIN SEARCHED KELLY'S computer, first skimming her emails, but nothing stuck out. Some were personal correspondence with friends, excited chatter about the upcoming wedding, which confirmed Fisher's story that Kelly still planned to marry him. Other notes were to vendors finalizing arrangements for the ceremony and reception. The emails were dated the day before Kelly disappeared, also confirming that she didn't have plans to run away or cancel the wedding.

A note from someone named Eleanor Goggins asked if she was going to attend their high school reunion. Two others girls, Anise Linton and Mona Pratt, had joined that discussion, all commenting on how much fun it would be to get the old crowd back together again.

He checked Kelly's financial records. Her account was stable, most transactions relating to household bills and payments to vendors. A large deposit had been added a week before from her father, which was probably meant to cover wedding costs. But nothing out of the ordinary.

He checked her browser history and found wedding decoration and planning sites, then noted she'd researched teaching positions and had sent applications to three different schools in Austin.

All confirmed Fisher's story.

Next he examined her social media sites. She was on Twitter, Facebook, Goodreads and Pinterest. He took a few minutes to skim her posts and discovered she liked mystery books and classics, and she tweeted and wrote Facebook posts about her job search and upcoming nuptials. Photos of her and Raymond filled her Facebook page: shots of them at college football games, hiking and sipping drinks on a beach vacation trip and engagement pictures taken at a mountain cabin.

Nothing suspicious. In fact, everything supported Fisher's and Lambert's story.

Amanda appeared from the bedroom, her expression troubled.

"What?" he asked.

She glanced at the patio and seemed to be relieved that Fisher was outside. "My deputy called. He found Kelly's car."

Justin arched a brow. "Where?"

"Out on Old River Mill Road." She lowered her voice. "It appears someone ran her off the road. Deputy Morgan found blood on Kelly's seat and paint from another car on her Toyota."

Justin's jaw tightened. "Someone intentionally ran her off the road, then abducted her?"

"That's what it looks like. I'd like to go out to the site and see for myself."

"Do you know what kind of car hit her?"

She shook her head. "No idea of the make and model yet, but it was pewter gray. Hopefully the crime team can tell us more from the paint sample."

"What kind of car does Fisher drive?"

"A black Lexus. There was a picture of him and

Kelly washing it." Amanda's expression softened. "They were laughing, covered in soap bubbles."

He closed the laptop. "I didn't find anything out of the ordinary. Let's go see her car, then we'll question the ex-boyfriend. If he drives a gray car, he might be our perp."

Justin's nerves jangled. He hoped to hell the ex was the man they were looking for. They might have a chance of getting Kelly back.

If not, she might disappear for months or years… or forever…like some of the other victims. And her father and fiancé might never know what happened to her.

AMANDA AND JUSTIN left with a word to Fisher that they'd keep him updated. Without even discussing the situation, they silently agreed not to tell him about finding Kelly's car.

"What kind of car does Mr. Lambert drive?" Justin asked as Amanda drove toward Old River Mill Road.

"A silver Mercedes."

"So far, Fisher and Lambert's stories hold up."

A sense of trepidation overcame Amanda. The image of Kelly's wedding dress hanging in the closet taunted her. Poor Kelly…she had been excited about her wedding.

And now it may never happen….

Night shadows hovered along the road, a breeze stirring the dead leaves and blowing them across the road like tumbleweed. Everything was dry this time of year, the temperature chilly.

Deserted land and cacti sprang up, making her wonder why Kelly would have been driving out on Old Mill River Road. Where had she been going?

Had she been planning to meet someone? If so, whom?

And why out here in the middle of nowhere?

Amanda wound down the road, noting signs for rental cabins along the creek a few miles to the north, but spotted her deputy's car ahead and pulled over.

"Why was she out here?" Justin asked as he climbed out.

She grabbed two flashlights, tossed him one, then retrieved her camera and a crime kit. "I was thinking the same thing." She spotted the red Toyota down in the ditch. Her deputy walked toward them along the side of the road. "How did you find the car?" she asked.

"Tracked her cell phone." Deputy Morgan held it up in his gloved hand. "Battery was low but it was still on."

"Did you check her call history?" Amanda asked.

Deputy Morgan glanced at the Ranger, then at her, and Amanda realized she hadn't introduced them. She quickly covered the bases and tugged on gloves

"Did you get anything from the phone?" Justin asked.

"Her last call was to a girl named Anise yesterday about ten a.m. After that, there were dozens of messages from the father and fiancé."

Amanda took the phone and clicked to listen to a couple. Each message sounded more frantic and panicked. "Fisher and Lambert both sound worried," she said.

"What about texts?" Justin asked.

Amanda checked the text log. "There's a couple from Fisher. He sounds more and more anxious as the night wore on."

"Fits with what they told us," Justin commented.

She continued to scroll backward. "Wait a minute. There's one here that came in yesterday about nine a.m. It's from someone named Hailey. She asked Kelly to meet her at the cabins I saw on that rental sign. Something about a surprise for her fiancé."

"We need talk to her. She may have had the last communication with Kelly."

Amanda handed him the phone. "You want to call the tech team and have them trace that text?"

"Sure." He glanced at the deputy. "Did you call a crime team in?"

The deputy nodded. "They should be here any minute."

Amanda tried to recall if there had been a girl named Hailey in their graduating class, but couldn't remember one. Maybe Kelly had met her at college instead of in Sunset Mesa. Or maybe she was a real-estate developer or event planner.

She shone her flashlight along the road as she

followed the deputy, her heart hammering when he pointed out the blood trail near the car. Determined not to miss anything, she snapped photos of the car and surrounding area.

The driver's door was open, the front window and bumper smashed, the weeds and brush crushed from the weight of footsteps—or a body.

Blood dotted the front seat and was splattered against the steering wheel.

But there was no sign of Kelly anywhere.

Except for her purse. It had fallen onto the floor, probably from the impact. Kelly's lipstick, wallet and compact, along with other miscellaneous items, had spilled across the mat.

Amanda picked up the wallet and looked inside. Driver's license and credit cards intact. Fifty dollars.

Not a robbery.

A cold chill swept over Amanda.

Judging from the blood on the seat, Kelly *was* injured. Although the amount of blood didn't suggest there was enough blood loss to kill her.

But since had been injured, she'd been easy prey, too weak to fight off a kidnapper or escape.

## Chapter Five

Justin looked up and down the road while he waited on tech to check the phone records. The tire marks needed to be photographed and studied—maybe they could discern the make of the car from the prints.

They might even get lucky and find some forensics evidence to help them.

The tech cleared his throat into the phone. "Okay, the text from Hailey came from a burner phone. There's no way to trace it or find out who bought the phone."

Dammit. "What about the fiancé's phone records? He said he received a text from Kelly saying she was going to spend the night with a friend named Betty Jacobs. But Betty said she didn't come over. Did Kelly call the Jacobs girl?"

A slight hesitation, and Justin heard computer keys tapping, then the tech's voice again. "There's a minute-long call to Betty Jacobs yesterday morning about eight o'clock but nothing afterward."

Justin headed down the hill to examine the car,

noting the blood splatters on the car door. "Check Fisher's records."

Another moment passed and Justin reached Amanda. She and the deputy were searching the trees surrounding the car crash.

He shone a flashlight and caught sight of a partial footprint to the left, then noticed a stiletto heel stuck in a patch of weeds.

"Sergeant Thorpe," the crime tech said. "I just examined Fisher's phone and you won't believe this, but the text that Kelly received from the burner phone—well, that came from the same phone that sent the message to Fisher saying Kelly wouldn't be home that night."

"So Kelly didn't send that text to Fisher. The kidnapper did."

"I'm surprised Fisher didn't notice that the number was different."

"There are a lot of their friends in town for the reunion. Maybe he thought she was using one of their phones."

The facts clicked together in Justin's mind, giving him a good idea of what had happened. He told the tech to keep looking at all the phone records from Lambert, Fisher and Kelly, then hung up and called out to Amanda.

"Did you find something?" Amanda asked.

"A shoe." He pointed to the foliage and Amanda raced over, then knelt to examine it. Her gaze shot back and forth from the car door to the wooded area and the trail leading back up to the road. "The driver hit Kelly's car, then dragged her from the crash and forced her into his vehicle."

Justin nodded. "That's how it appears." He sighed. "I just talked to tech. The text Kelly received asking her to meet this person Hailey was sent from a burner phone."

"So Hailey could be a fake name?"

"Probably. The text Kelly supposedly sent Fisher saying she was going to her friend Betty's house for the night—that was a fake. It came from the same burner phone."

Amanda ran a hand through her hair. "I assume there's no way to trace the number?"

"Afraid not. The texts were obviously a setup."

Amanda winced. "Someone lured her out here with the intention of kidnapping her and doing God knows what else." She gestured toward a shoe in the bushes. "The question is why? And if he went to all that trouble to lure her out here, then our unsub targeted her specifically."

He admired her logical mind. "That's true. Up until now, we wondered if the victims were chosen randomly. Now we know that someone specifically wanted Kelly Lambert."

"But who?" Amanda asked. "So far Mr. Lambert and Fisher seem to be telling the truth."

"Let's talk to Kelly's ex-boyfriend," Justin said. "Maybe he wanted her back badly enough to kidnap her."

AMANDA CONSIDERED HIS comment. It was a very likely scenario. Especially if Terry Sumter was obsessed with Kelly and was desperate to win her back.

Although they had to look at all angles.

"That's a possibility," Amanda said. "But there's another one that might fit."

"What?"

"Maybe another woman wanted Raymond and decided to get Kelly out of the way so she could move in on him."

Justin frowned. "We'll talk to Kelly's girlfriends and Fisher's male friends. Hopefully one of them can give us some insight there." He gestured toward the car. "We might luck out and find a print or hair that the kidnapper left behind."

The sound of an engine rumbling echoed from the road, and they all climbed the hill together. The crime van rolled up, techs spilling out with their kits. Amanda thanked the deputy and asked him to go back to the office to man the phones and follow up with the bank. By now, Kelly's photograph should have gone into the system. They could only hope someone would call in with a lead.

Another officer brought a police dog and began to search the area.

The head of the unit introduced himself as Lieutenant Gibbons, then pointed out the other workers by name. A redheaded woman named Petunia, a chubby guy named Larry, a rail-thin guy with funky glasses named Jerry, and the guy with the dog was named Herbert.

Amanda explained what they'd discovered so far and handed over the shoe to be bagged and sent to the lab. The next hour they scoured the area in case Kelly had somehow escaped, but finally even the dog team gave up.

"We'll take a cast of the tire print," Lieutenant Gibbons said. "And we're going over the car with a magnifying glass."

"Run the paint sample through the lab, too," Justin said. "Maybe the paint was custom designed for a particular vehicle."

Amanda checked her watch. "It's getting late, but I want to talk to the bridal party tonight." She removed her phone and called Fisher. "Call everyone in the bridal party and tell them to meet me at the sheriff's office in half an hour."

"Did you find something?" The young man's voice warbled as if he'd been crying.

"We'll talk when Sergeant Thorpe and I get there."

She disconnected, dread balling in her stomach. Telling Kelly's fiancé and father about finding the car would be difficult. If they'd harbored any shred of hope that Kelly had simply gone away for a couple of days without telling anyone, the fact that they'd found blood would kill that hope.

JUSTIN STUDIED THE group of young men and women who'd gathered in the sheriff's office.

Kelly's bridesmaids and best friends—Betty Jacobs, Anise Linton, Mona Pratt and Eleanor Goggins—were all attractive women in their twenties, although they were a mixture of brunettes, blondes and redheads.

Any one of them could have fit the profile of the victims who'd disappeared over the past few years. So far, the kidnapper didn't have a clear MO, which had slowed down the police in connecting the cases in the beginning. Normally a kidnapper/killer chose a certain type—all blondes or brunettes or redheads. This unsub seemed to have no preference for hair color or body type or career choice.

Except they were all in their twenties and lived in Texas.

The groomsmen looked nervous as they settled into wooden chairs. Glenn Cates, Danny Latt and Lance Stephens. Fisher's father, Ernie, was his best man. He stood beside his son with a hand on his shoulder.

Raymond looked even worse tonight, the strain of the day wearing on him.

Amanda had taken Kelly's father to her back office to explain to him about the car and their findings.

"I want to thank you all for coming," Justin said.

"Did you find Kelly?" Mr. Fisher asked.

Justin shook his head. "I'm afraid not, but we did find her car."

Raymond jerked his head up, while the others exchanged worried looks.

"Where?" Ernie Fisher asked.

"Out on Old River Mill Road."

"What was she doing there?" Raymond asked.

Justin crossed his arms, studying the group for their reactions—any sign that one of them might have already known about the car. But he caught no signs of deceit on their faces, only fear and worry.

"Our tech department studied the text that you received, Mr. Fisher, the one supposedly sent from Kelly telling you she was spending the night with Betty."

"What do you mean, 'supposedly sent'?"

"That text was sent from a burner phone, not from Kelly's. That same phone sent a message to Kelly asking her to meet the person out on Old River Mill Road."

Fisher's eyes widened in horror. "Someone tricked her into going out there."

"That's correct," Justin said. "Whoever it was sent you that text so you wouldn't realize she was missing until the next day."

Gasps and whispers rumbled through the group.

Raymond paced over to Justin, his breath wheezing out. "Someone kidnapped her, didn't they?"

Justin swallowed hard. "It appears that way, Mr. Fisher. Her car had been run off the road and crashed into a ditch. We also found a small amount of blood on the seat."

Fisher's face crumpled with emotions. "Oh, my god. She might be…hurt or gone like those other women."

"Why her?" Betty sniffled. "Everyone loved Kelly."

"She was so excited about her wedding," the girl named Anise said.

"And the shower," Eleanor added. "She couldn't wait to open the gifts and move into her new house."

Mona wiped tears from her eyes and hugged Eleanor.

Justin made a low sound in his throat. "Can any of you think of anyone who'd want to hurt her?"

Heads shook, mumbled nos resounding through the room.

Amanda stepped from the back with Lambert who looked ashen-faced and distraught. "Please call us if you receive a ransom call," Amanda told him.

He nodded, then looked over at Fisher, pain radiating from him. "Have you heard anything, Ray?"

Raymond shook his head no, rubbing his bleary eyes.

Amanda rapped her fingers on the desk. "Ladies, I'd like to talk to you individually."

"And I need to interview each of the groomsmen," Justin added.

Mumbled questions and protests sounded.

One of the groomsmen, Lance, scowled, his arms crossed. "You think one of us had something to do with her disappearance?"

"That's not what we're implying," Amanda cut in. "But you might be able to help in some way. You *do* want to find Kelly, don't you?"

Heads nodded, everyone piping up with yeses.

Amanda gestured toward Betty. "Why don't you come with me first? It'll only take a few minutes." She glanced at Justin. "You can use my deputy's office to interview the men."

Justin pointed to Raymond. "Come on, Fisher. There are a couple of things I need to ask you."

He looked sullen and nervous, but he followed Justin without a word. The moment Justin shut the door, the man turned on him.

"What else can I tell you? I don't know who would send me and Kelly that text. And I sure as hell don't know anyone who'd want to hurt her."

"Mr. Fisher," Justin said calmly. "You mentioned that Kelly's ex wanted to get back with her. I'm going to question him as soon as I leave here. But Sheriff Blair pointed out another possibility."

He hesitated, giving the man a moment to gather himself. "Do you have any ex-girlfriends that were unhappy about your upcoming wedding? Maybe a woman who wanted to get back with you? Or…one who wanted to get revenge against you for some reason?"

Fisher lapsed into a stunned silence for a moment, then dropped into a chair. "I don't think so…I mean…"

"What? There's something you remember?"

Fisher wiped his forehead with the back of his hand. "I did break up with my old high school girl-friend to date Kelly our senior year," he said. "But that was ages ago. Renee wouldn't do anything to hurt Kelly because of it. She's probably already moved on."

Justin gritted his teeth. "Where does she live?"

"Some small town north of here." He drummed his fingers on his knee, thinking.

"What else?"

A muscle twitched in his jaw. "She chaired the committee to set up the high school reunion."

"So she knew you were coming back for the re-union and to get married. Perhaps facing old friends as a single woman while you two were together pushed her buttons?"

"I suppose it's possible," Raymond said, but he didn't sound convinced. "Although I just can't imag-ine it."

Justin shoved a pad toward him. "Write down her contact information. You do have it, don't you?"

A sliver of guilt streaked the man's face. "Yes, but only because of the reunion."

"Right." Justin watched him scribble the woman's name and number, wondering if she could have kid-napped Kelly out of jealousy.

Now they had two feasible suspects, Kelly's ex-boyfriend and Raymond's ex-girlfriend.

His cell phone buzzed, and he checked the num-ber. The ME.

"Excuse me," he told Fisher. "I have to take this. You can go now."

Fisher looked wary as he rose. "You want one of the other guys sent in?"

Justin nodded. "Send Lance Stephens in." He'd start with the guy who'd protested. Maybe he had a reason to avoid questions.

His phone buzzed again, and he hit Connect. "Sergeant Thorpe."

"It's Dr. Sagebrush. We have an ID on the body from the creek."

Justin held his breath. "Her name?"

"Tina Grimes."

"Cause of death?"

"As we first thought—strangulation," Dr. Sagebrush said.

"Any sign of sexual assault?"

"No, she wasn't raped," Dr. Sagebrush said. "But there's something else that I noticed, too. I don't know if it's important, but her high school class ring was clenched in her hand."

Justin frowned. What did that mean? That she'd hung on to it as the perpetrator killed her?

Or had the perp put it in her hand as part of his signature?

The yearbook annuals were all laid out in a row on the top of the dresser. All the high school students from Sunset Mesa, four years' worth of girls who'd finished their high school degrees and gone on to plan their futures.

They were successful, married, had babies of their own. One had even become a reporter who covered human-interest stories.

Ironic since the little witch had no sense of humanity.

Flipping the pages brought a sea of females who had to be punished.

Amanda Blair's photograph stood out. She wore her softball uniform and was grinning from ear to ear after Canyon High won a game. Amanda had been a star player.

She'd also abandoned one of her friends, someone who'd needed her.

And she would have to be punished for that.

But there were others that had to be dealt with first. So many others…

Who would receive their penance next?

## Chapter Six

Amanda had interviewed two of the bridesmaids and had two more to go. According to Betty and Anise, Kelly adored Raymond, couldn't wait until the wedding and had intentionally planned the ceremony the week after the reunion so more of her former classmates could attend.

Amanda studied Mona, aware the blonde was only a year younger than her. Man, she felt old. More worried about dead bodies and missing young women rather than a date for a mani-pedi and highlights.

"Did you sense any trouble between Raymond and Kelly?" she asked.

Mona twisted a strand of hair around one finger, reminding Amanda of the way the girl had behaved in high school. She had been a huge flirt. All the guys had eaten out of the palm of her hand.

"They were the perfect couple," Mona said, blinking back tears. "I just can't believe she's missing."

"Raymond said that her ex-boyfriend, Terry

Sumter, wanted to get back with her. Did she mention that to you?"

Mona sighed. "She said she'd heard from him, but she blew it off. Every couple of years, Terry would contact her and want to get together, usually after he'd broken up with his latest conquest."

Amanda zeroed in on her word choice. "Conquest?"

She laughed softly. "Yes, he could be charming, and whenever he met someone new, he poured it on. But eventually the girls wised up to his slick moves. When he was drinking, he had a bad temper. That's why Kelly broke up with him years ago."

"Did he ever get physical with her?"

Mona chewed her lip as if debating on her response.

"Mona, just tell me the truth. If you think he might have hurt Kelly, I need to know."

"Well, I can't imagine him actually kidnapping her. But Eleanor and I saw him at the pub one night and he was pretty trashed, mouthing off. He blamed Kelly for his life falling apart."

"Falling apart?"

"Yeah, he said she abandoned him, and after that his life spiraled downhill. Said he'd always wanted her. When she left, he didn't trust women anymore."

"That was her fault?"

"According to him, yeah. I think he just lost his job, too."

"What did he do?"

"He worked in construction. I think he was about to get his own crew," Mona said. "But it wasn't Kelly's fault he lost his job. He probably got caught drinking at work."

Maybe. Still, if he blamed Kelly for his problems, maybe he had come after her to get revenge.

JUSTIN FINISHED INTERVIEWING the three groomsmen, not surprised that the men all vouched for Raymond. After the phone call identifying Tina Grimes, he was looking for a connection between the two cases. But Raymond had no reason to hurt Tina.

Of course the killer, Raymond or otherwise, could have murdered Kelly, hoping the police would assume she'd been taken by the same perp who'd kidnapped the other girls.

Glen Cates and Danny Latt had attended high school with Kelly and Raymond as well as Amanda, and, as teens, had formed a bond that, according to them, could not be broken. Lance Stephens had met Raymond in college and they were frat brothers, making their bond just as tight.

They also adamantly refuted the suggestion that Kelly might have cheated on Raymond, saying she was as devoted to him as he was to her.

Justin had never experienced that kind of devotion and wondered what it would be like.

*Dammit, don't let the case get to you. You like being alone.*

Sure, occasionally he wanted a hot body to warm

him at night. Amanda's sexy face flashed in his mind, and for a brief second, he allowed himself to indulge in the idea of taking her to bed. Stripping her naked and tasting every inch of her. He'd bet his next dollar that she'd be as fiery and passionate in the sack as she was about police work.

But reality interceded. Facing the same woman day after day wasn't on the agenda.

His job was his wife.

And the last thing he needed was to get his butt fired for making advances toward a female sheriff. These days a man had to be careful.

Had to protect his reputation.

He'd learned a long time ago that the only person he could count on was himself.

Turning his thoughts back to the case, he left the men in the front office, strode to the back and knocked on Amanda's door. A second later, she opened it, ushering the young woman named Eleanor out.

"I've finished with the men," he said.

"Let's send them all home and interview Kelly's ex-boyfriend, Terry Sumter."

He agreed, but as his gaze met hers, his earlier thoughts taunted him. He'd tried to ignore those enormous eyes before, but now they intrigued him. Made him wonder what had made her so tough… and sexy at the same time.

An incredibly lethal combination.

She grabbed her jacket, and he dragged his mind away from sex and to the case.

"Thanks for coming in, everyone," Amanda said. "Go home and get some rest."

"Just let us know if you hear from Kelly," Justin said.

Bleak faces stared back, the young women's expressions full of fear as if they realized that they could become a victim just as easily as Kelly had. Especially if this criminal was choosing random women.

But he'd intentionally avoided linking Kelly's disappearance to the others to avoid panic.

Raymond stood on shaky legs. "Please find her, Sergeant Thorpe and Sheriff Blair."

Justin nodded and Amanda murmured she'd be in touch.

Raymond's father guided his son out, talking in a hushed voice, trying to offer words of comfort that Justin was certain fell on deaf ears.

"God," Amanda said as the door closed and they were left alone. "I'm afraid we may not be able to give him what he wants."

Justin gritted his teeth. He knew exactly what she meant. Because Fisher wanted his fiancé back alive, saying her vows at their wedding. He and Amanda both knew that might not happen.

He might be burying her instead.

That is, if they found her body. So many victims had never been found or their bodies recovered.

Amanda rubbed the back of her neck, and he realized she looked tired. Hell, she was probably exhausted. It had been a long day.

And it wasn't over.

Justin propped one hip against the desk. "We need to talk before we go."

A streak of panic darkened Amanda's face, and she poured another cup of coffee. She handed him a cup, then took hers and sank into her desk chair with a resigned sigh as if she knew he had bad news.

"The medical examiner called. They identified the body from the creek. Her name was Tina Grimes."

The color faded from Amanda's face, emotions clouding her eyes for a minute. "Jesus."

"You knew her?" he asked softly.

She nodded, then shoved a strand of hair away from her cheek. She was such a tough woman, but that one gesture seemed utterly feminine and made her look vulnerable.

Made him want to pull her into his arms and console her.

"We went to grade school together, then high school," she said. "Tina was a year ahead of me. The last time I saw her was at her mother's funeral."

And now she would have to attend Tina's.

"Were you good friends?" Justin asked.

"Not really. Tina was popular, more of a girly girl. Me…I was a tomboy."

"You played sports," he said, not surprised.

"Softball and I ran track and was on the swim

team." She rolled her shoulders. "My father once asked me if I wanted to try out for cheerleading and I said, 'Why would I cheer for a bunch of boys when I could play my own sport and people could cheer for me?'"

In spite of the somber mood, Justin chuckled. He liked Amanda more and more every second.

Dangerous.

"Her father will be devastated," she said lost in her thoughts.

He simply nodded, giving her a moment to assimilate her feelings.

Finally she gave him a determined look. "Cause of death?"

He tapped his foot. "Strangulation. Killer used a belt. No sexual assault."

She sipped her coffee, mulling over that information. "So the killer is not driven by sex."

"Or he's impotent," Justin offered. "Although it could also suggest that the killer is a female. Strangulation is a common choice for murder with females. It also usually implies that the kill was personal."

Amanda jerked her head up. "Then again, we don't know if Kelly's disappearance is related to Tina's yet. They attended the same school but the first girls who disappeared did so as teens. Kelly is in her twenties."

Justin nodded. But there were too many disappearances for them not to be connected.

They just hadn't found the connection yet.

"We need more information," Justin said. "Who investigated Tina's disappearance?"

"The former sheriff, Lager. But I inherited the files." She rose, reached for a whiteboard on a swivel stand and turned it to face him. His eyebrows shot up. She had methodically listed each disappearance over the past nine years in chronological order along with details of the individual cases.

A map also showed highlighted markings. "The green indicates where the girls lived, the red is where they disappeared from or were last seen."

He studied the map, searching for a commonality. "The first two victims were Melanie Hoit and Avery Portland. Both grew up in Sunset Mesa although Melanie moved to Amarillo after graduation and was last seen at a shopping mall. Tina lived in Sunset Mesa at one time, as well."

He checked the map for Carly Edgewater and Denise Newman. "What about Carly and Denise? They went missing from neighboring counties. Did they ever live in Sunset Mesa?"

Amanda flipped through the file on her desk. "Hmm, Carly did when she was younger. She and her parents moved to Austin when she was fourteen."

"And Denise?"

She skimmed another file, her mouth thinning into a frown when she looked up. "Actually she lived here for a couple of years when she was fifteen.

When her parents split, her father took her to a small town east of here."

She tapped the folders. "If all the girls lived here at one time, then Sunset Mesa is the connection."

"It looks that way."

"But why? What about this town triggered the unsub to kill?"

Justin remembered the rest of his conversation with the ME. "Dr. Sagebrush found a high school class ring in Tina's hand."

"So you think—"

"That whoever is taking or hurting these young women targeted your residents, specifically ones who attended Canyon High."

Except that Carly and Denise hadn't.

What the hell was going on?

JUSTIN'S WORDS REVERBERATED over and over in Amanda's head. "You're right, but at least two of the victims didn't go to the high school."

"They must have crossed paths with the perpetrator when they lived in the town though, enough for the killer to track them down."

She'd looked at each victims' past boyfriends, girlfriends and family problems, even issues at a job where the women could have made enemies, but found nothing to link them.

Still, she couldn't deny the truth—they had a serial kidnapper/killer in Sunset Mesa.

Were all the victims dead?

Whoever it was could be holding some of them hostage. But why? If he didn't want sex, what was his motive?

*It could be a woman.*

Although the percentage of women serial killers was so small that that scenario wasn't likely. But it was possible.

So far, they hadn't had a single person come forward claiming to have seen one of the abductions.

The person who'd taken Kelly had been smart and used texts to lure her to an isolated area. Maybe he'd done that with the others, as well. But he would have had to send the text as someone the girls trusted.

"The high school ring in her hand," Amanda said, thinking out loud. "That must be significant. Most of us stopped wearing them once we went to college."

"Right. That's normal."

"Kelly and Raymond planned the wedding shortly after the reunion so old friends could attend." Amanda's stomach roiled. "And with everyone coming back into town, that means the killer might be looking for another victim now."

SUZY TURNER HAD to die next.

She had been nothing but a two-faced, lying slut. Had stolen other girls' boyfriends and lied to her friends' faces. She'd worn short skirts to show off her long legs and tops that were three sizes too small and dipped down to her navel so all the guys would be drawn to her chest.

Yes, she had wanted attention, had craved having a trail of guys lusting after her and she'd teased them unmercifully, then made fools out of them so everyone in school would know.

The teenagers these days, the bullies, often showed up at school with guns and wiped innocents out while they exacted their revenge on the guilty and the ones who stood by and let it all come to pass.

But that wasn't the plan here. The plan was to eliminate the ones who'd been cruel. The ones who'd humiliated the geeks and nerds, the guys who hadn't been born with muscles and impeccable looks.

Yes, Suzy had been a bad, bad girl.

The door to her house stood open. She had a pool in back. She was out there now, skinny-dipping as if she didn't have a care in the world.

Little did she know that it would be her last swim.

Tonight she would say goodbye to her pitiful life. And all the world would be better that she was gone.

# Chapter Seven

Justin didn't like the direction of his thoughts.

He jumped into his vehicle, antsy with the latest revelations. If someone was targeting young women from Sunset Mesa, especially ones around Amanda's age, then she might be in danger.

They needed to figure out the suspect's motive. Were there specific women being targeted or were all of the women who'd attended the local school in jeopardy?

For God's sake, with the reunion in less than a week, the kidnapper/killer could be stalking his next victim. And if that was the case, they would be hearing about another missing woman—or finding another body—soon.

He couldn't let Amanda out of his sight.

But if the unsub was targeting specific females from Canyon High, they needed to figure out the reason he was choosing those particular victims.

"We need to look at all the victims again, detail everything we know about them and see if there's a pattern. If they fit a type."

"They were all popular, well-liked cheerleaders, on the dance team, or color guard." Amanda frowned as she buckled her seat belt.

"So our killer doesn't like cheerleaders or dancers? That seems thin." Justin tapped his foot. "Was there any one male or female who hated all of them for some reason?"

"Not that I can think of. Of course there were typical girl rivalries but nothing that stands out."

"Like the bus accident in Camden Crossing?"

"Exactly. That incident changed the town. There were a lot of angry parents and friends. No one suspected that the soccer coach had been sexually harassing and assaulting the girls on his team."

Justin contemplated her statement as he veered onto the road leading to the apartment complex where Sumter lived. "How about any parties where things went wrong? Drugs? Kids getting arrested? A boy accused of rape by one of the girls?"

Amanda rubbed her temple. "I don't remember anything like that."

She fell silent for a moment, her brow furrowed.

"What?" he asked.

"Now that I think about it, there were two things that happened. Donald Reisling had a bad car accident his junior year and has been in a wheelchair ever since."

"What happened?"

"He was supposedly driving drunk, but there were

rumors that his girlfriend at the time was behind the wheel, and that he covered for her."

"What happened to the girl?"

"She moved away after college, but I saw that she'd RSVP'd that she planned to attend the reunion."

"What about Donald?"

"He was pretty broken up. His family was irate. They tried to prove the girl was behind the wheel, but her father hired a fancy lawyer and the case was dismissed." Amanda pointed to a sign indicating the turnoff for the complex. The area was rundown, the concrete building outdated.

Odd for a man who was supposedly a builder himself.

"Donald's in a wheelchair, paralyzed from the waist down. There's no way he's strong enough or physically able to kidnap and kill anyone, then dispose of their bodies without someone noticing."

Justin turned into the parking lot, spotting a few battered cars, a black dusty Jeep, a Land Rover and a few pickup trucks holding supplies, obviously used for work.

"Unless he has a partner."

Amanda's eyes widened. "I suppose that's possible."

"What about his family? They have to harbor ill feelings about the court decision."

Amanda seemed to stew over that suggestion. "I

don't know. I haven't seen him in years. But I know Donald's father still lives outside Sunset Mesa."

"And you said the old girlfriend is coming back for the reunion?"

Amanda sighed, sounding distressed. "Yes, her name is Lynn Faust. She's on the committee that organized the dinner dance."

Justin made a clicking sound with his teeth. "Maybe this reunion stirred up resentments. The father could be bitter that his son has spent the last few years in a wheelchair while this girl went on with her life. And now she's throwing it in his face that she's returned to dance at their reunion when he can't even walk."

"My God, you could be right. That might explain why Tina was left holding the class ring. But why kidnap or kill the others? Why not just go after the woman who ruined Donald's life?"

"Perhaps Donald or his father's resentment has grown, so he views all the victims as hurting Donald. After he was in the wheelchair, he probably didn't get many dates." Justin scraped a hand over his chin. "Lynn could be his endgame."

Fear streaked Amanda's face. "We need to warn her."

Justin shook his head. "Let's talk to the father first and test our theory. We don't want to cause unfounded panic."

She nodded although she fidgeted, obviously still worried.

He veered into the parking space, rolled to a stop, then cut the engine. "You said there were two incidents."

She shrugged. "The other was a suicide, a guy named Carlton Butts."

"What happened?"

Guilt flashed in her eyes. "He was a friend of mine," she admitted softly.

"You dated?"

"No. Nothing like that." Amanda bit her bottom lip. "He was a smart kid, but a nerd," she said. "I don't mean that in an ugly way, but he was one of those kids who was teased a lot. I… We grew up together and hung out some because I wasn't popular either."

Justin's gaze met hers. "I find that hard to believe, Amanda."

The vulnerable look on her face moved something inside him. Could she not see how beautiful she was? That he was turned on by her tough, stubborn drive and intelligence?

"IT'S TRUE," SHE said, hands clenched. "But the difference between me and Carlton was that he cared and I didn't." Her voice dropped to a pained whisper. "I should have realized how deeply his depression ran. But it was spring and I was caught up in softball and swim meets."

A well of sadness and grief once again assaulted Amanda as she thought about Carlton. He was a classic case of a quiet kid with brains whose gangly body and glasses had caused him to be the butt of jokes from the testosterone-laden guys and silly teenage girls who'd treated him as if he was nothing.

Not that he was the only kid who'd been picked on. Which had made her wonder why he'd chosen suicide when he'd had a bright future and probably would have garnered college scholarships from more than one university.

"Amanda, his death wasn't your fault."

Justin's gruff voice made her glance across the parking lot. She couldn't look at him when she felt so raw. Exposed.

Guilty.

"Maybe not," she said. "But I should have been a better friend."

"I'm sure you *were* a good friend," he said. "But none of us can really know what's going on in another person's head unless they tell us."

She absorbed his words, knowing that on a rational level, they were true. But they still didn't alleviate the regret that filled her soul.

"Is Carlton's family still in town?"

She swallowed the lump in her throat. "His mother is. But she's not doing well. I think she has some kind of degenerative disease, bad rheumatoid arthritis. She has to use a walker to get around."

"Any other family?"

"A brother. Actually, he and Carlton were fraternal twins, as different as night and day."

"The brother was popular?"

"Yes. He was a wrestler so girls liked his body. He lives in a neighboring town."

"Were he and his brother close?"

Amanda wrinkled her nose. "Not really. I always got the impression they didn't get along, that Carlton's brother was impatient with him. He wanted Carlton to stand up for himself."

Justin narrowed his eyes. "Did the sheriff investigate the kid's death to make sure it was a suicide?"

"Not really," Amanda said. "Carlton's brother was away at the time at a wrestling tournament. And Carlton left a suicide note so no one really questioned it."

"Hmm. I'm still surprised there wasn't an investigation."

"I guess they had records from the shrink Carlton saw confirming his depression."

Justin reached for the door. "All right. Let's take it one step at a time. First Kelly Lambert's ex. Then Fisher's. Then we'll question Donald Reisling and his father."

Amanda climbed out, her nerves on edge. This case was even bigger than she'd first believed.

She just hoped they figured it out before anyone else died.

Justin checked his weapon to make sure it was secure and hidden beneath his jacket as he and Amanda walked up the sidewalk to Sumter's apartment. All this time they'd wondered if the missing girls were connected and looked for a psychopath who simply liked to kidnap young women.

But now they might have a lead. If the kidnappings/kills were personally motivated, finding the original trigger was the key to stopping the crimes. With the upcoming reunion, the killer had a whole pool of victims at his fingertips.

Whoever it was obviously had a bone to pick with the women in Sunset Mesa and was making a point.

He glanced at Amanda as she knocked on the door to Sumter's apartment. "Mr. Sumter, it's Sheriff Blair and Sergeant Thorpe," she yelled through the door. "We need to talk to you."

Justin kept his eyes peeled around the outside of the string of units, searching for trouble. If Sumter knew they were asking questions and he was the perp, he might ambush them.

Or he might have gone into hiding.

There were dozens of places in the deserted area surrounding Sunset Mesa to lie low and stay off the grid.

They waited for several seconds; then Justin raised his fist and knocked louder. "Mr. Sumter, if you're in there, answer the door."

"Were you friends with this guy?" Justin asked.

Amanda shook her head no. "Terry and Kelly were tight their freshmen and sophomore years. He was a big jock, but he had a cocky attitude." She gave a self-deprecating laugh. "Besides, by then

I was more interested in the cases my father was working. I used to quiz him all the time."

"What about your mother?"

Sadness flickered in her expressive eyes. "She left when I was fourteen. Said she couldn't take wondering if he was coming home at night any longer."

Justin understood that kind of worry, that marriage for lawmen was near impossible. The reason he'd avoided it altogether. No reason to put a woman or himself through the pain when things fell apart.

And things always fell apart.

"But what about you?" he asked. "Why didn't she take you with her?"

A self-deprecating laugh rumbled from her throat. "She said she knew I'd choose Dad, and she wasn't going to make me choose." She shrugged. "Maybe she was right. I don't know."

"But you wanted them both," he said, understanding. "Do you keep in touch with her?"

Her jaw tightened. "She remarried, has another family now."

A wealth of hurt underscored her words, but he didn't reply because shuffling sounded inside the condo. Feet pounded. Something slammed, like a window or a door.

Justin's senses jumped to full alert.

"He's trying to run," he muttered.

He slammed his shoulder against the door, knocking the thin wooden frame askew. Then he pulled his gun and rushed in, Amanda behind him.

A noise from a back room made him jerk his head to the right, and he ran toward the bedroom. The window was opening, wind swirling through the room. He rushed to it and saw Sumter climbing into the bushes. "Stay here and look around. I'm going after him!"

Not bothering to wait for her response, he ran back through the den and outside. He veered around the side of the building, then saw a figure dive from the bushes below the window and take off toward the woods in back.

"This is Sergeant Thorpe, Sumter. Stop. I'm armed." He sprang into motion and chased the man as he jumped a pile of trash in his backyard. "You're not going to get away!" Justin shouted.

The man tripped over something and nearly fell, but caught himself, glanced back and continued to run. Justin picked up his pace and caught up with him within seconds. He jumped him from behind and threw the man to the ground.

"Get off of me, I haven't done anything wrong," Sumter growled.

"You ran," Justin snapped. "That makes you look guilty."

Sumter spit on the ground as Justin dragged him to a standing position and shoved him back toward the building. Sumter smelled like booze and cigarette smoke and cursed as Justin forced him back into the apartment.

Amanda stood in the den, her expression angry. At him or Sumter?

He didn't have time to analyze it.

Justin shoved Sumter toward the couch, which was piled high with dirty laundry. The scruffy man collapsed on it with another round of expletives.

"You have no right to barge in here and harass me," Sumter muttered.

"We have every right," Justin said coldly.

Amanda crossed her arms and stepped in front of Sumter, staring down at him.

It made her look sexy as hell, but Justin refrained from commenting out loud.

"Why did you run, Terry?" Amanda asked.

"I thought you were a burglar," Terry said sarcastically.

Justin shook his head. "We identified ourselves."

"You know why we're here," Amanda said.

For a brief second, pain flashed in the man's eyes, before a smirk replaced it. "Yeah, I know, *Amanda.* You think that you're better than the rest of us now because you have that badge."

Justin squared his shoulders, irritated at the sarcasm in Sumter's tone.

He'd wondered if some of the younger people in town resented having one of their classmates assume the sheriff's position.

"I am better than you, Terry, because I'm not a drunk," Amanda countered.

He shot to his feet, rage seething from his every pore. "You bitch."

Justin shoved him back down. "You make another move toward her and your butt will be in jail."

Sumter made a low sound in his throat, then snapped his mouth shut.

"We have to ask you some questions about Kelly's disappearance," Amanda said calmly, showing no trace that his attitude affected her.

Sumter scowled at them, then scraped a hand through his already tousled dirty-blond hair. "I don't know anything."

Justin took a quick inventory of the inside of the apartment. It was just as rundown as the outside. Faded paint on the walls, worn furniture and stained carpet. The place reeked of cigarette smoke, stale beer and fast food.

A coffee cup filled with muddy sludge sat on the chipped coffee table and unwashed dishes filled the sink.

The man was not only a drunk but a slob.

"We heard that you wanted to get back with Kelly," Justin cut in sharply.

"I had a thing for her a while back," Sumter said, tugging at his ratty T-shirt. "But I've had other women since."

"Still, you wanted her back," Justin said. "Her fiancé told us that."

Sumter's eyes narrowed to slits. "She was too good for that jerk."

"He seems nice to me," Amanda said. "Like he really loves her."

"*I* loved her," Sumter said. "And she promised to love me forever. Then Fisher stole her from me."

"We were just kids back then, Terry," Amanda pointed out. "Everyone moves on from that first love."

Terry glared at her through glazed eyes. The man must have been sleeping off a hangover when they'd knocked. And the place reeked of pot.

Perhaps the reason he'd run?

"But you didn't move on, did you?" Justin asked.

"Yes, I did. I told you I've had other women." He smiled, a cunning evil in his eyes. "In fact, I don't have trouble in that department."

"Having other women doesn't mean you forgot Kelly or that you stopped wanting her." Justin took a menacing step toward him. "The reunion was coming up and so was Kelly's wedding. You figured you'd make one last attempt to win her back, so you called her and asked her to meet you."

Terry dropped his head slightly. "I did ask her, but she had other plans."

"Plans that didn't involve you. Plans to marry Raymond Fisher," Amanda said.

Justin poked Sumter with his finger. "That made you even angrier, didn't it?"

Amanda's voice hardened. "So you sent her a text

pretending it was from someone else and lured her out to the Old River Mill Road."

"I did no such thing," Sumter snapped.

"You ran her off the road, then dragged her from the car," Amanda continued.

Terry shook his head no, his expression adamant. "No…"

"What kind of car do you drive?" Justin asked.

Terry glanced back and forth between them as if he suspected they were trying to trap him. "A pickup truck," he said. "I use it for work."

"What color is it?" Justin asked.

"Black," Terry said. Realizing he might be in serious trouble, he gave Amanda a pitiful, lost-boy look. "Amanda, you really can't think I'd hurt Kelly. You've known me for years. You know I'm not capable."

"I know you have a temper when you're drinking," Amanda said. "And judging from your breath and the empty bottles in your kitchen, I'd say you've been doing a lot of that."

"Did you know Tina Grimes?" Justin asked.

Sweat beaded on Terry's forehead. "Tina? What the hell are you asking about Tina for?"

Amanda folded her arms across her chest. "She also went missing months ago—"

"Jesus, you think I took her and killed Kelly?" Sumter's panicked gaze darted toward the door. "Hell, you're crazy, Amanda. I'm not some serial nutcase."

"Just answer the question," Justin said firmly.

Terry clamped his mouth shut. "I'm done talking. I want a lawyer."

SUZY TURNER WAS such a stupid bimbo. She had fallen for the plan with no questions asked. Had even been friendly.

Friendly after what she'd done.

The sick bitch.

Her body now lay limp, her ivory flesh red and bruised where the belt had tightened around her throat.

Now, what to do with the body?

For so long the others had lain hidden inside the town. No one knew where they were, that they had never really left Sunset Mesa.

But now everyone had returned to town to celebrate, to relive their old high school glory days.

They had to see what had come from those days. That they hadn't been so glorious at all.

That not everyone felt like celebrating.

And it was time for them to pay for their sins.

## Chapter Eight

"What do you think about Terry?" Amanda asked as they drove back to the sheriff's office.

Justin worked his mouth from side to side. "He looks good for Kelly's murder, but I'm not sure he fits the profile of a serial criminal. He's too out of control with the drinking."

"I agree. As volatile as he is, he would get sloppy and would have made mistakes by now."

"Maybe leaving Tina's body so it could be found was a mistake."

"True. But still, our killer has to be more organized, methodical."

"You're right." Justin glanced at the clock on the dash. "It's nearly midnight, Amanda. Let's call it a night. It's too late to visit Fisher's ex-girlfriend."

Amanda twisted her hands together. "I hate to go to bed knowing we haven't found Kelly."

Justin recognized a faint hint of despair in her voice and wanted to assure her they'd find the woman. But there were too many others missing that they hadn't yet located, so he couldn't make false promises.

"I understand," he said instead. "But we've done all we can today. Her picture is being run nationwide. Police everywhere are searching for her. You need to get some rest and we'll go at it again tomorrow."

Amanda nodded. He was right. But she wasn't sure she could sleep when images of Tina Grimes's dead body floated in her head.

Was Kelly going to end up like that?

Was she still alive?

Justin parked, and the two of them climbed out and went inside. Darkness bathed the streets, most of the residents in the sleepy little town tucked in bed for the night.

But were they safe?

It was her job to make sure the residents were protected.

What if she failed?

JUSTIN HAD WORKED in law enforcement long enough to know that Amanda was taking this case personally. As they entered the police station, she poured herself another cup of coffee.

And why wouldn't she take the case personally? She'd known some of the victims. She knew Kelly Lambert.

And now it seemed that members of her high school were being targeted by a serial criminal.

She was probably racking her brain to figure out the reason.

Meaning she probably wouldn't sleep tonight.

"Have you eaten anything today?" he asked.

She looked at him as if he'd grown a second head. "I can't even think about food."

"Amanda," he said, his voice softening at the tortured look in her eyes. "You can't do your job if you don't rest and eat something. Is there anything open this time of night?"

"No."

"Do you have food at your place?"

She shrugged. "Eggs, I guess."

"Okay. Everything in the inn and hotel was booked, so I'm probably going to sack out in your jail. Let me follow you home and I'll make us an omelet while you grab a shower. With something in your stomach, maybe you can sleep and think more clearly tomorrow."

"You don't believe I'm thinking clearly?" she asked, her tone defensive.

"That's not what I meant." He released an exasperated sigh. "But once you relax, once we both do, maybe you'll remember something, or I'll come up with a more concrete theory than we already have."

In fact, he planned to spend the night studying the background and files on each of the cases. They had to be missing something.

She glanced at the files on her desk, then stuffed them in a worn shoulder bag. "All right, let's go.

But you're not staying in the jail. You can sleep on my couch."

He started to argue, but she threw up a warning hand. "Trust me, it's not that comfortable, but it's better than one of the cots in the cell."

He conceded with a nod. "All right. I want to talk to Renee Daly in the morning. Then question Donald Reisling and his father."

He gestured for her to lead the way, and he followed her outside. She locked the office, then climbed in the sheriff's car while he followed her in his SUV.

She lived about a mile away in a small neighborhood with a mixture of older brick, stucco and adobe homes. Most looked well kept, the yards manicured, flowerbeds blooming. Judging from the kids' toys in the yards, it was a neighborhood of young families.

"Why did you choose this neighborhood?" he asked as he followed her up the cacti-lined walkway. Was she planning a family?

"It was close to town and affordable." She unlocked the door. "You'll have to excuse the mess. I don't have company very often."

Was that her way of telling him she didn't have a boyfriend?

"Hey, I'm not complaining. Like you said, anything's better than the prison cots."

In fact, he liked her place immediately. It was rustic inside, homey, with soft leather couches, throw pillows and folk art on the walls. The kind of place a man felt comfortable in, not one of those frou-frou women's showcase homes where the furniture was meant to be looked at but not touched.

He'd once dated a woman with white couches. Who the hell had white couches?

She flipped on a lamp, bathing the walls in a golden glow, then dropped her bag on a desk in the corner. His gaze was drawn to the sultry sway of her hips as she walked to the adjoining kitchen. Even though she was in uniform, he could tell she had enticing curves beneath the plain fabric.

Obviously exhausted, she released the ponytail holder keeping her hair from her face, and shook the wavy strands free.

Unexpected desire instantly bolted through him. The gesture seemed somehow intimate. Although she didn't seem aware of what she was doing to him. The scent of some kind of feminine spray, maybe a body wash, blended with vanilla.

"Want a beer?" she asked, one hand on her hip as she stopped by the fridge.

"Sure." She grabbed two from the refrigerator, popped the top on both of them and handed him one while she took a long pull of the other.

His gut tightened as he watched her tip the bottle back. Her slender throat worked to swallow the cold liquid. Then she flicked out her tongue to lick her lips and raw need seized him.

Damn. He wasn't supposed to be attracted to her. She was a sheriff, for God's sake.

But she was still a woman. A very sensual one.

"Go shower," he said, desperate for her to leave the room so he could regain his composure. "I'll whip up an omelet."

She studied him for a long moment, an odd look in her eyes. Friendly? Wary? "I've never brought a man here," she admitted softly.

So she didn't have a boyfriend?

Ridiculous, but relief made him smile.

"Of course this is just work," she said. "Maybe we can review the files while we eat."

Disappointment tapped at his desire.

Hell, though, not enough to destroy it. He still wanted her.

Sex was the best stress reliever.

But how would she feel if he suggested a one-night stand? No complications, just hot, raw sex.

*She'd probably slug you, sue you for sexual harassment and laugh in your face.*

"Sure, just go shower," he said a little more sharply than he intended.

Her eyes flickered in confusion, but she shrugged it off a second later and made her way down the hall.

Traitorous thoughts of her naked in the shower with rivulets of water streaming down her bare back pummeled him. The sound of the shower kicking on taunted him with what-ifs.

What if they weren't working a case and they'd just met in a bar and shared a night of passion?

Dammit to hell and back. It did no good to torture

himself with the idea of holding her and tasting her. He needed a distraction.

Food. He needed to concentrate on the food he could eat and the investigation.

Sweat beading on his forehead, he scrounged through her refrigerator, hoping an omelet would satisfy this sudden unsettled feeling clawing at him.

Because bedding Amanda was not an option.

IN SPITE OF the hot water, Amanda shivered. Had she misread that hungry look in Justin's eyes a few minutes ago? Her body tingled as the soapy bubbles coated her skin and the water sluiced over her bare breasts.

Heat speared her as she imagined Justin stripping and stepping into the shower with her. His fingers would trail over her naked skin, making her body come alive with desire.

Desire that would bring them both pleasure as they slid their naked bodies against each other, then melded their mouths and tasted the heat simmering between them.

His hands would skate over her back, then lower, over her hips and she'd open wide for him. He'd lift her and she'd impale herself on his rigid length. He would feel so good inside her....

Struggling for control, she ducked her face beneath the water.

Good heavens alive. The tension of the day had

definitely gotten to her. She was not the kind of girl to fantasize about sex.

Especially with another law officer.

She would ruin her career forever if she let him know how she felt.

Furious with herself, she scrubbed her body and hair, then rinsed, climbed out and dried off. Whistling a tune her father used to hum beneath his breath, she towel dried her hair and slid on a pair of shapeless sweatpants and a long sleeved T-shirt. Nothing that looked remotely sexy or inviting.

Not that Justin was interested. Was he?

*He's a man. Men are always interested in sex.*

But there would be nothing more than that, and she couldn't indulge in a one-night stand with a co-worker.

Heck, she'd tried to be a modern woman and pretend sex wasn't personal, but she couldn't do it. Her emotions always got in the way. Besides, she couldn't give her heart away and chance having it broken.

She tousled her damp hair with her fingers, then headed back into the kitchen. The scent of bacon and eggs filled the space, and her stomach growled. When she entered, Justin had set the table with two of her mismatched plates and poured them both orange juice.

She set the rest of her beer on the table and noticed that he'd opened a second one. Hot buttered toast sat in a stack on another plate in the center of the table. He scooped the bacon on a paper-toweled plate, then flipped one omelet, then another, onto their plates. He'd obviously raided her refrigerator and found the green peppers and mushrooms in the crisper.

"You were pretty stocked," he said.

She sank into the chair, suddenly ravenous. "I enjoy cooking when I have time. I have a bad habit of making up my own recipes though."

"Sounds creative. This is about my limit," he said. "Although I can grill a mean steak."

Her mouth watered, but just as much for him as the steak.

Their gazes locked for a heartbeat, a moment of charged heat rippling between them. Her nipples hardened as if he'd touched them, and arousal speared her.

"Amanda?" he said in a gruff tone.

"It looks great," she said, pasting on a cheery smile to diffuse the tension. "Let's eat."

She dug in with gusto, and he did the same, both obviously deciding to ignore the moment.

Amanda spotted her series of yearbooks on the bookshelf by the fireplace in the den, retrieved the last two years', then started flipping through them while she ate. Justin finished off his meal and took another swig of his beer.

She pointed out some random shots of the football games, cheerleaders and pep rallies.

"Here are Avery and Melanie," Amanda said. "They were the first two girls to disappear." She flipped the page to a shot of Kelly, Anise, Mona and Julie Kane, the prom queen. "All these girls were friends."

"What about Renee Daly, Fisher's ex?"

Amanda searched the photos and frowned as she found a candid of Raymond and Kelly beneath the big tree where the students used to gather to talk. "Here she is." In the background, Renee Daly stood by the breezeway shooting daggers at the couple.

Was she jealous enough to carry a grudge all these years? And if so, why not just go after Kelly to begin with? Why carry out a ten-year-old vendetta?

Serial killers often came from abused families. None of these girls fit that description and neither did Terry Sumter or Donald Reisling.

She flipped to another page, her pulse hammering at the sight of Donald Reisling in his wheelchair at a basketball game. He was sitting all alone beside the bleachers, his expression angry as if he had no friends.

Because they'd abandoned him. "Now that I think about it, some of the girls said their parents didn't want them hanging out with Donald, not after they knew he'd been driving drunk."

"Did he go to college?"

Sympathy for Donald mingled with suspicion. "He lost his basketball scholarship. I heard he went to some kind of technical school, maybe on the internet."

She pointed to the front row of the bleachers.

"That's Lynn Faust beside Jimmy Acres. He took over the lead spot on the basketball team after Donald was paralyzed."

Could Donald or his father have hated Lynn and the other girls for turning their backs on him after the accident?

Hated them enough to kill them?

## Chapter Nine

Justin wrestled with images of Amanda all night while he tossed and turned on her couch. Maybe it would have been better if he'd stayed at the jail.

No woman had ever made him lose his focus before. He couldn't afford it this time either. Innocent women's lives depended on him.

His phone buzzed, and he reached for it, the nerves along his neck prickling. It could be news of another body or another missing woman.

But it was his superior, Chief Stone Stabler.

"Morning, Chief." He rose and went to look out the kitchen window. Last night it had been dark when they'd arrived and he hadn't noticed the view out back. The sun rising over the canyon took his breath away.

This must be the reason Amanda had bought the house. The canyon loomed behind her, vast, rugged and beautiful.

"Where does the case stand?" Chief Stabler asked.

"We think that the disappearances are all related to Sunset Mesa. So far, most of the girls attended the same high school. The ones who didn't lived here at one time. The body discovered in the creek belonged to a woman named Tina Grimes. Her class ring was found in her hand."

"Any suspects?"

Justin spread the pictures of the missing women across the desk in the corner. His gut told him yes. "I think so, but I'll know more after I finish questioning some of the locals."

"All right. How is it working with that sheriff? Is she cooperating?"

Justin swallowed back an image of her in the shower, the one that had kept him awake half the night. "She's fine. Competent." And sexy as all get out.

They agreed to talk later and disconnected; then he scribbled a note to Amanda saying he'd meet her at the station. He was going to notify Tina Grimes's father that her body had been found.

He quickly dressed, then went through the drive-in doughnut shop for a doughnut and coffee. Thirty minutes later, he knocked on the door of Mr. Grimes's house.

It was a nice Georgian home on an estate lot in the next town. Colorful flowerbeds adorned the front lawn, twin lion statues flanking a water fountain in the center of the circular drive.

He rang the doorbell, his mouth tasting gritty. This was the worst part of his job.

A maid answered the door, so he flashed his

badge and identified himself. "I need to see Mr. Grimes please."

She mumbled, *"Si,"* then escorted him to a study to the right and disappeared. Justin scanned the library, noting that Grimes had a collection of antique books as well as travel and finance magazines.

Footsteps clattered, and an astute man with graying hair entered through the arched doorway. Age lines fanned his tanned face, and his clothing indicated he was dressed for a golf game.

Justin hated to ruin his day, but the man probably hadn't had a good day since Tina disappeared.

Grimes took one look at his Silver Star and paled. The man instinctively knew the reason he'd come.

"You found Tina?" he asked, his voice thick with desperation.

Justin nodded. "I'm afraid so. I'm sorry, Mr. Grimes."

Grimes stumbled toward his desk chair, then sat down and dropped his face into his hands. Silent sobs wracked his body, and Justin simply waited, giving him time to absorb the shock.

Finally Grimes heaved a breath, wiped his eyes with a handkerchief and looked up at him. "Where?"

"In Camden Creek."

"Did she...suffer?"

He grimaced. The man didn't need to know details. "She was strangled."

"God..." Another sob erupted, making Justin's heart squeeze with compassion.

Grimes looked up at him with tear-filled eyes. "Do you have any idea who did it?"

"We're working on a couple of leads." He hesitated, leaned forward and steepled his hands. "I understand you're grieving, sir, but I need to ask you a few questions."

A weary sigh reverberated from the man. "I already told the sheriff everything I knew months ago."

"I understand. But we found a high school class ring from Sunset Mesa in Tina's hand. Was the ring special to her?"

Grimes pulled at his chin. "We moved here from Sunset Mesa her senior year. She didn't graduate from Canyon High."

"Did she keep in touch with her old friends there?"

He hesitated, thinking. "Some of them. Kelly Lambert and Suzy Turner. She and Suzy went to college together."

Justin's mind raced. "How about old boyfriends from Canyon High?"

Grimes rose, went to the bar and poured himself a scotch even though it was barely breakfast time. Under the circumstances, Justin cut him some slack.

After Grimes downed the scotch, he turned back to Justin. "Before we moved, she dated a guy named Donald. But he broke up with her to date some other girl. I think he ended up in a wheelchair, some drunk-driving accident."

"Did she keep in touch with Donald?"

"He called her a couple of times after the accident, but he was a wreck. And since he dumped her, she didn't take him back."

Motive for Donald.

"Thank you, Mr. Grimes. And again, I'm sorry for your loss. The ME will contact you about retrieving Tina's body for burial."

At his words, the man broke down again.

He laid his card on the desk. "Call me if you think of anything else that might help."

"Please, Sergeant Thorpe," the man said, his voice filled with anguish. "Find out who did this to my little girl."

Justin met his gaze. "Don't worry, sir. I intend to."

Justin let himself out, climbed into his SUV and phoned the ME. "Dr. Sagebrush, did you find any DNA on that class ring in Tina's hand?"

"I was just about to call you," Dr. Sagebrush said. "As a matter of fact, I did."

Justin's pulse jumped. This could be the lead they needed. "Whose was it?" The man who abducted and strangled her?

"That's the interesting part," Dr. Sagebrush said. "I thought it might be the killer's, but it's not a male's DNA. It's a female's."

Justin sucked in a breath. "Do you have a name?"

"Melanie Hoit," Dr. Sagebrush said. "The DNA

belonged to one of the first women to disappear. Also, I found her initials inside the ring."

The ring didn't belong to Tina as he'd originally thought.

Justin's fingers tightened around the phone. That DNA meant that the cases were connected. The killer had taken Melanie's ring and placed it in Tina's hand as his signature.

To taunt them with the fact that he'd been abducting and killing young women and getting away with it for years.

And he obviously wasn't finished.

BY THE TIME Amanda met Justin at the sheriff's office, she'd reviewed the missing-persons files again and combed through her yearbook.

She hated the fact that every face she saw now looked like a suspect. The mayor had also called for an update on the Lambert case, pushing her to make an arrest, and two reporters had called, requesting an interview.

She passed Julie Kane driving toward the school on her way to the office and was tempted to pull her over and warn her that a madman might be after her and their classmates.

But that would cause panic. She needed more information first.

She was on her third cup of coffee when Justin strode in. Wow. The man looked as if he'd grown another inch. He'd shaved, too, although she had to admit she'd liked his five o'clock shadow. Still, she wanted to run her hands across his jaw and feel those big arms of his flex beneath her touch.

Lack of sleep. That was the only explanation for her racy thoughts.

"Morning," he said in a deep, throaty voice. A voice laced with fatigue that told her he hadn't slept any better than she had. Of course, he'd probably been focused on the investigation, not fantasizing about her.

That thought burst her bubble, and she handed him some coffee. "Are you ready to question Fisher's ex?"

He gave a clipped nod. "Yes, but I have some information for you first."

A shiver rippled up her spine at his tone. "What?" Please not another dead body.

"I talked to the ME. He found some DNA on the class ring Tina Grimes had clenched in her hand."

That was good news. "Who did it belong to?"

"Melanie Hoit."

Questions pummeled Amanda. "I don't understand. Melanie disappeared years ago. How could Tina have her ring?" The truth dawned, ugly and disturbing. "The same person abducted both of them."

He nodded.

Amanda rubbed her arms with her hands. "Do you think Melanie is still alive?"

"I doubt it," Justin said, his expression grave. "The killer probably took Melanie's ring as some kind of trophy. He may have kept all his victims' class rings as souvenirs."

His theory made sense. She'd heard of serial killers personalizing their MOs. "But we haven't found any other bodies. And Tina didn't graduate from Canyon High."

"Her father said she dated Donald before Lynn did, and that he contacted Tina after the accident, but she wouldn't take him back."

So all roads were leading back to Donald.

"The unsub has been lying low, picking off these young women one at a time. For some reason, they all spark his hatred or anger, probably of a specific woman who hurt him."

"And the reunion triggered him to escalate," Amanda said, following his logic. "The perp has stayed off the grid all these years, but this ten-year reunion means something to him. It's an anniversary of sorts."

"Exactly. He can't stand the thought of everyone gathering to party and celebrate their accomplishments when he feels hurt, betrayed by them."

"When his life didn't work out the way he wanted," Amanda said, thinking of Donald. She hated to suspect him after all he'd suffered.

But she had to do her job.

Justin gestured toward the door. "Let's go talk to

Renee Daly. Then we'll confront Donald Reisling and his father."

He was right. Donald had good reason to hate Lynn Faust. He could be taking all his rage out on the other girls who had shunned him and still be planning to kill Lynn.

Probably on the night of the reunion.

They walked to his SUV in silence, but as soon as they settled inside and she gave him directions, she voiced her concerns. "Justin, maybe we should plan a press conference for the town. Warn the women that they're in danger."

"They probably already realize that," Justin said. "Besides, all we have is a working theory now. No proof."

"No, but if the reunion is his trigger, he may strike at one of the events. I should tell Julie Kane and the other organizers to call off the events until we catch the killer."

"Continuing with the events might be the best way to trap this guy," Justin said as he made the turn. "We can assign extra law officers to watch for trouble."

Amanda's stomach somersaulted. That was a good, solid plan. Except that it meant endangering more women.

Women she knew personally, had known most of her life.

Not that they were best friends, but she'd sworn

an oath to protect them and Justin's idea would do the opposite.

"Think about it," Justin said. "We have a couple of days to figure it out. Maybe we'll get lucky and catch the suspect and the reunion plans can go on without a hitch or panicking the town."

AMANDA WAS WORRIED about the residents in town.

But he was worried about her.

Until he knew the unsub's specific motive, and whether or not Amanda was on the hit list, she wasn't leaving his side.

"There, Renee works at the dress shop on the corner," Amanda said. "She has a boutique that supposedly sells the latest designer wear."

He shot her a wry look. "In Sunset Mesa?"

Amanda chuckled. "I know. This little town is old-school Western all the way. She wants to class it up."

Amanda was probably the classiest thing they had.

She indicated the corner down the street on the left, and he drove past the bank and diner. Kelly Lambert's father was exiting his Mercedes and entering the bank, but his shoulders were hunched, and he looked tired as hell.

Another night where his daughter hadn't come home.

And they had no good news to tell him.

Justin parked in front of the boutique, noting the

short skirts and five-inch heels in the window. For a brief second, he wondered what Amanda would look like in nothing but those heels.

Oblivious to his wandering thoughts, Amanda shoved her door open and slid from the seat. The sign on the shop door indicated it didn't open until ten, but he could see movement in the back through the front window.

Amanda rapped on the door. "Renee, it's Sheriff Blair. We need to talk to you."

A heartbeat passed; then footsteps tapped on the floor inside. A woman's voice answered, "Hang on," and the door opened. A bell tinkled above them and Renee, a tall, leggy blonde wearing a miniskirt and tube top that looked absurdly out of place in the small town, appeared.

Justin had to admit she was attractive, but she did nothing for him. Didn't stir his hunger like Amanda did in her dull uniform.

"What's going on, Amanda?" Renee's eyes darted from Amanda to him, obviously curious.

"Renee, this is Sergeant Thorpe of the Texas Rangers. We need to talk to you about Kelly Lambert's disappearance."

A frown pulled at Renee's eyes, barely registering on her Botoxed forehead. "I heard about that. It's awful," Renee said. "Do you have any idea who abducted her?"

Amanda gave her a deadpan look. "Not yet. We're

talking to everyone who knew her and trying to piece together what happened."

"You used to date her fiancé, Raymond Fisher?" Justin cut in.

Renee rolled her eyes. "Yes, but that was ages ago. We're just friends now."

"So friendship is all you wanted from him?" Amanda asked.

Renee looked shocked at the implication that she might want more. "Of course. I have boyfriends in three different cities. I don't need an old high school tagalong."

"Are you seeing anyone specific now?" Justin asked.

She lifted a blood-red fingernail and raked it along the buttons of his shirt. "Not anyone serious. How about we get together later for a drink?"

Amanda stiffened beside him.

Justin clenched his jaw. Most men would have been pleased at her advance. But Justin was simply annoyed. He wrapped his fingers around her hand and stopped her playful tease.

"No, thanks. We're working a case," he said. "Do you know anyone who would have wanted to hurt Kelly?"

Renee shook her head. "No. But poor Raymond. I bet he's distraught."

"Yes, he appears to be," Amanda said.

Renee's eyes twitched with a devilish gleam. "I guess I'll have to console him at the reunion."

Justin's stomach twisted. He really didn't like women like Renee. Teases. She probably flirted with anything in pants.

"What about that dead girl they found at the creek?" Renee asked. "I heard she used to live around here, too."

"She did," Amanda said. "Other women in Sunset Mesa have disappeared over the past decade, too, and we suspect it might have something to do with our class. That our reunion might be triggering someone's anger toward the females."

Renee paled, and she stepped backward, her hand gripping the door. "Are you saying this maniac might come after me?"

THE TEENAGERS OF Sunset Mesa would wake up today, wolf down breakfast, go to school and find one of their alumni lying on the bleachers waiting for them.

Kelly Lambert didn't look so pretty right now.

Getting her onto the football field had been an ordeal. But it was worth it.

Maybe the bullies and mean girls would think twice about how they hurt others the next time.

Yes, all the members of that class were counting down the days till they partied together again.

But their party might be moved to the cemetery when they realized how many of them would end up dead.

## Chapter Ten

"What did you think of Renee?" Amanda asked, hoping the sliver of jealousy she'd felt when the wicked woman had flirted with Justin hadn't shown through.

She had no reason to be jealous. Justin was his own man. He could flirt or sleep with anyone he wanted.

They weren't even remotely involved and never would be.

"I think she's a big flirt and probably a liar. But that also tells me she probably wasn't serious enough or obsessed enough with Fisher to carry a ten-year-old torch for him."

"True, she has always been superficial," Amanda said, surprised but relieved that Justin hadn't fallen for the woman's charm. Most men did.

"I also think she's too concerned with fashion, her looks and appearances to dirty herself enough to commit a murder." Justin folded his hands, flicking his fingernails. "Did you see those fake claws?

Girls like that are too worried about breaking a nail to strangle someone."

Amanda laughed. "You're right. Let's go talk to Donald."

"His home or work?" Justin asked.

"I looked him up this morning. He has a home office, works in computer graphics."

She gave him the address and pointed out directions as he drove. But her nerves remained on edge as they passed the high school, and she saw teachers arriving for work, buses beginning to pull up. The marquis out front announced that prom was fewer than two weeks away. The same night Kelly's wedding had been scheduled. Amanda wondered if she'd planned it that way.

The reunion date was also posted.

A bad feeling crept over her, and she clenched the seat edge. Had something else happened?

"Is this the right road?" he asked.

"Yes." Amanda pointed to the subdivision. "Go to the end of the road and turn left."

He pulled down the row of houses, all older with a spattering of well-kept single-family homes mingling with rentals that had seen better days. He turned left and they wound down a mile-long private drive to the Reisling estate.

Justin parked and Amanda caught his arm before they got out. "If you don't mind, let me take the lead. Donald might be...defensive."

"He also might be guilty," Justin said. "I don't intend to cut him any slack just because he's in a chair."

"Fair enough," Amanda said, although her heart squeezed. She felt like Donald had been dealt a shoddy deal in life.

Yet he'd chosen to say he was driving instead of turn Lynn in.

He'd probably regretted that a thousand times over. If so though, why hadn't he changed his testimony later?

The enormous estate house sat on several acres, grandiose and stately.

"What the hell does this man do to own this place?" Justin asked.

"Family money," Amanda said. "Donald's father is an entrepreneur, works in investments and has done well. But Donald's grandfather invented some kind of farm equipment that he patented and it earned them a fortune."

Justin followed her up to the door, where she rang the bell. A few minutes later, a voice sounded and the door opened to reveal Donald in his wheelchair.

But instead of looking scruffy and angry, as if he was living in the past, he was well dressed in dress slacks and a blue shirt and his hair was groomed.

"Amanda?"

"I'm the sheriff now," she said.

"That's right, I heard that," he said, his mouth quirking to the side.

"This is Sergeant Thorpe with the Texas Rangers," she said. "Can we come in?"

"Sure. What's this about?"

"Kelly Lambert's disappearance."

"That was shocking. I don't know how I can help, but come on in." He turned and wheeled his way through the two-story foyer to an office equipped with a state-of-the-art computer system.

Reisling parked his chair behind his desk and indicated a coffee decanter on the sideboard. "Help yourself."

Amanda and Justin both declined. Her gaze was drawn to the high school trophies on a bookcase behind him. If his basketball career hadn't been cut short, he would have most likely added college ones to that collection.

"Donald, when was the last time you saw Kelly?" Amanda asked.

Donald rubbed his temple as if he had to think about the question. Because he was fabricating a lie?

"Honestly, it's probably been months. She dropped by one day to ask me if I wanted to help with the committee organizing the class reunion." He grunted. "Imagine that."

Justin cleared his throat. "Sheriff Blair told me what happened years ago. Her visit must have angered you."

Donald chuckled. "Actually I thought it was funny. I asked her why she thought I'd even want to attend, much less help organize the thing. It's not like I've stayed friends with anyone from back then."

Anger hardened his tone. She couldn't blame him. Hadn't she thought the same thing when she'd opened her own invitation? And she didn't have the reason to dislike their classmates that he did.

"So why didn't you move away?" Justin asked.

Donald shrugged. "Takes money to have a place set up for handicap access," he said matter-of-factly. "I'm not proud that I live at home—then again, my father is rarely here. He has his own office and travels. And I stay in the guesthouse. He also fronted me startup money for my own business. Now, I'm doing pretty well," he said. "I've been looking at buying a condo in the city."

Amanda offered him a smile. "It sounds like you've made a success of yourself." Not as if he was stuck in the past.

He gave a sarcastic laugh. "Business is good. But not a lot of women can handle the chair."

Sympathy for him stole through Amanda.

"Where were you day before yesterday?" Justin interjected.

Donald's expression turned to steel. "What? Why? You don't think I had something to do with Kelly's disappearance, do you?"

The strained second that followed answered his question.

He cut his eyes toward Amanda. "Amanda, why would you think that?"

"You suffered a terrible tragedy and got the raw end of the deal. Everyone said Lynn was driving the night of your accident."

"That must have eaten at you all these years," Justin said in a dark voice. "Watching her go on with her life, date other guys, have everything you missed out on with no consequences."

Any semblance of friendliness faded from Donald's face. "Even if I did harbor resentment toward Lynn, why the hell would I hurt Kelly?" His voice rose an octave. "Besides, I thought some sicko stalker was kidnapping those women."

Justin crossed his arms. "It's possible that the kidnapper hates all women who remind him of the one who first hurt him."

Tension stretched between the two men as Donald realized the implications of Justin's statement.

Donald pressed a hand over his chest. "Look, that person is not me. I decided a long time ago that anger was only holding me back."

"That's very mature of you," Justin said.

Amanda pursed her lips. "So you forgave Lynn?"

"Yes." A mixture of emotions seethed in Donald's eyes. "You may not believe me, but look at me." He gestured at his chair. "Even if I wanted revenge or was this sick person you're talking about, how the hell would I kidnap anyone and get away with it?"

"Donald, we're just trying to get to the truth,"

Amanda said calmly. "One of the missing women was found in Camden Creek. She'd been strangled and was holding one of our class rings."

"So you think someone in our class murdered her?"

Justin spoke up. "Someone who had a beef with the females. After your accident, we heard that the girls turned you down for dates."

Pain wrenched Donald's eyes. "I admit it was a rough time, but that doesn't make me a killer."

"We're talking to everyone still in town and everyone coming in for the reunion," Amanda said.

"What about your father?" Justin asked.

A muscle ticked in Justin's jaw. "What about him?"

"You may have forgiven Lynn and accepted your situation, but did he?" Justin asked. "He probably enjoyed watching you play basketball. He had big dreams for you. Then those dreams were crushed because some teenager caused your paralysis. That would be enough to set off any parent."

Donald gripped the wheels of his chair and flew around his desk. "I think you need to leave now."

"Please, Donald," Amanda said. "If you know anything about Tina's death or Kelly's disappearance, tell me. I don't want to see anyone else hurt."

Donald gestured toward the door. "I told you what I know. Now, if you want to talk to me again, go through my attorney."

"I WANT TO talk to Reisling's father," Justin said as they left the estate.

Amanda fastened her seat belt. "He has an office in town."

"You feel sorry for the guy, don't you?" Justin asked.

Amanda twisted sideways to look at him. "I don't know what to think. If he's truly forgiven Lynn, then maybe he's found some peace and happiness and he's not our perp."

"But his father might be," Justin pointed out. "A parent's love is the strongest bond there is. I've seen fathers, especially fathers of athletes, do outrageous things to help their kids succeed."

"I know there are stories of fistfights at little league games, and dopers at the Olympics—"

"And parents who sought revenge against another person for hurting their child."

Amanda bit her lip as they lapsed into silence.

Ten minutes later, they arrived at Reisling's office on the corner of town. Justin faintly wondered why the man hadn't kept his office at home as his son had, but figured Reisling had other employees working for him and needed a professional space.

He was worried about Amanda, too. Knowing the people in town made it more difficult for her to treat them as suspects.

She obviously hadn't seen the harsh realities he had on the job. Teenagers killing their parents. Husbands and wives taking out hits on one another.

Babies abused and children mistreated in heinous ways.

"Were you and Donald friends growing up?"

Amanda shook her head. "I told you before, I wasn't in the popular crowd. He was."

"Until the accident," Justin clarified. "Coupled with the loss of his scholarship, losing his social status and the extra burden of helping him start his business, his father could have broken."

Amanda sighed wearily. "I know logically you're right. But it's hard for me to believe that a serial killer has been living in Sunset Mesa all this time and no one caught on."

Justin wanted to cut her some slack. "Sometimes people are blinded because they're too close to the situation."

"To see the forests for the trees," Amanda finished. "But surely a friend or family member would have noticed something suspicious."

Justin parked, noting as they walked up the sidewalk that the office space was the nicest building on the street. Reisling must have spent some major bucks on renovations. "It's possible that the killer lives alone. Or that if a family member noticed something suspicious, he or she is in denial."

Amanda sighed. "Or they feel indebted enough to the unsub not to turn him in."

He reached for the door to the office. "That would fit Donald. He has to feel indebted to his father."

"I don't like this," Amanda said. "But I like even

less the fact that a killer might have been hiding in town right under my nose."

Justin squeezed her arm. A dangerous move because heat blazed through him instantly. Amanda glanced down at his arm, then licked her lips, drawing his gaze to her mouth.

Damn. She had luscious full lips. Lips he wanted to taste.

"Don't beat yourself up, Amanda," he said softly. "This string of disappearances started long before you took office. You were only a teenager back then."

"Yes, but when I think about my classmates, I can't imagine any one of them committing these crimes."

He dropped his hand and opened the door. "Let's talk to Reisling."

The inside of the office was plush and modern, nothing like the Western feel of the town. Steel gray and chrome furniture, a high-tech computer where a receptionist sat and expensive artwork.

He didn't feel as if he was in Texas anymore.

Amanda led the way to the receptionist's desk. "We need to talk to Mr. Reisling."

The middle-aged woman with platinum hair frowned up at Amanda, giving her a jolt of surprise.

"Mrs. Kane, I didn't realized you worked here." Or that she worked at all. She had been the country-club type.

"Yes," the woman said with a sheepish look. "I've

been here a couple of years now. Mr. Reisling's good to me."

Amanda glanced sideways at Justin. "Is he in, ma'am? It's important we talk to him."

Confusion marred the woman's face, which obviously had had some touch-up work. "Can I tell him what this is about?"

Justin flashed his badge. "Tell him it's urgent police business."

She rose, diamonds and jewels glittering, then disappeared through a doorway that probably led to more offices in the back.

"You seemed surprised to see her here," Justin said.

Amanda jammed her hands in the pockets of her jacket. "I am. She was one of those tennis moms who had maids and martini lunches."

Justin started to say something more, but the door opened, and Mrs. Kane waved them through, then led them into a hallway and to an office space that was even plusher than the entry and waiting area. The computer system outdid the sheriff's office's ancient one by thousands of dollars.

Mr. Reisling greeted them with shakes of their hands and indicated for them to seat themselves in the area in the corner. A sparkling water decanter sat by crystal glasses, along with a fancy espresso machine, and a fully loaded bar ran along the back wall. Reisling offered them a drink, but Amanda shook her head and Justin cut straight to the chase.

"Mr. Reisling, we're investigating the disappearance of several young women from this area over the past ten years, the most recent being Kelly Lambert. We also recently recovered the body of Tina Grimes."

Mr. Reisling smoothed a hand over his red tie. "I don't understand what that has to do with me." He glanced pointedly at Amanda. "What's going on, Sheriff?"

"A class ring from Canyon High was found in Tina's hand, Mr. Reisling. Added to the fact that all the girls lived in the town at one time and that the majority of the victims attended the local high school, we believe the abductor/killer is from this area. That he has some personal beef with these young women."

Reisling shook his head, his right eye twitching. "I still don't get why you're here."

"Because we know what happened to your son," Justin said flatly. "How unfair it was that he was permanently paralyzed and persecuted for driving under the influence when the girl that was with him escaped and then dropped him."

"Good God, that happened ages ago," Mr. Reisling said, his face reddening with anger. "And yes, I was bitter, sometimes still am bitter, because that little tramp lied and hurt my son. But—" he stepped closer to Amanda, eyes flaring "—my son forgave her and managed to make something of himself. So I'm incredibly proud of him."

"That doesn't mean you didn't harbor hatred for all the girls who turned him down for dates after the accident." Justin matched the man's intimidating stance.

If the guy laid a finger on Amanda, he'd deck him.

"Maybe I did hate them," Reisling said, his lips curled into a snarl. "But that doesn't mean I've been kidnapping or killing them! I'm a businessman and well respected in this town." He jerked his thumb toward the door. "Now, unless you're here to arrest me, get the hell out of here. And leave my son alone. He's suffered enough."

Amanda's phone buzzed, cutting into the tension, and she snatched it up and headed to the door.

Justin clenched his jaw. Reisling was the kind of man who used his power and money to get what he wanted. The man might not be guilty, but Justin didn't like him. Reisling was smart, calculating and, he suspected, vindictive.

If he was methodical in his business, he was probably also meticulous, organized and patient—patient enough to wait ten years to build toward his endgame.

AMANDA GLANCED AT the caller ID on the phone, surprised to see the number for Canyon High. Was this call about the reunion? Maybe the staff had heard about the discovery of Tina's body and decided they should postpone it.

"Who is it?" Justin asked.

"The school." She punched Connect. "Sheriff Blair."

"Sheriff, it's Principal Blakely at the high school. You need to get out here."

Amanda gripped the phone tighter. "What's wrong?" Not a school shooting. God, there were too many of those....

"This morning when our track team met at the track, they found a body on the bleachers in the stadium."

Amanda's legs threatened to buckle. "Who is it?"

"Kelly Lambert. She was murdered, Sheriff. Murdered and left here for the kids to find."

## *Chapter Eleven*

Amanda staggered toward the car. "Lock the school down, Principal Blakely."

"It's on lockdown and we've confiscated cell phones, but I can't say for sure that one of the students hasn't already texted or sent this out. There may be photos already on the internet."

Oh, God...

"We have to contain the situation," Amanda said. "Keep everyone away from the field. I'm on my way."

Her vision blurred with the mind-boggling implications of the phone call. "We need a CSI team at the school along with extra officers," she told Justin as he met her at the car.

"What's wrong?"

"Kelly Lambert's body was found on the high school bleachers in the football stadium."

Which meant everyone in the entire school needed to be questioned. And that whoever had killed her was ready to make a bolder statement...and to make that statement in a public way.

AMANDA'S FACE PALED as she disconnected, and Justin couldn't help himself. He reached out and steadied her with his hands.

"Amanda?"

"I have to see her family before word gets out about this. If it hasn't already."

"With teens and their cell phones, it probably is out," Justin said in disgust. "People have no respect for privacy anymore. The more morbid or shocking the better."

Amanda visibly shook herself as if to pull herself together. "We need to go."

"I'll call for backup and for a crime scene team," Justin said. "Hell, we'll need a whole crew to question all the students."

Her phone was beeping again and she checked it. "Dammit, it's Mr. Lambert."

"He knows." They jumped into the car, and Justin started the engine and headed toward the school.

"Sheriff Blair, Mr. Lambert—" A pause and Amanda massaged her temple with her fingertips. "I just heard, Mr. Lambert. I'm so sorry that you found out through a text."

Justin punched in his chief and explained the situation, and he agreed to send teams to help canvass the students. Phones would have to be kept, photographs of the victim and crime scene analyzed.

Had someone touched the body? Changed anything?

All details that would affect the investigation.

They could only hope a witness had seen the killer leaving the body...

No, the drop-off had probably been done during the night when the place was empty.

But...if the perp was getting daring enough to leave a dead victim at a public place, maybe he'd gotten sloppy and they'd find some evidence this time.

He glanced back at Reisling's business and wondered if the rich cocky jerk had been at the high school last night dumping Kelly's body.

Was Reisling cool enough to fake his calm when they'd arrived at his office?

"No, sir, you cannot come to the school," Amanda said. "The school is being locked down, Mr. Lambert. Police and Texas Rangers will be all over the place. I promise you I'll let you know as soon as we move her body so you can see her."

Justin heard the man's sobs as he ended the call. Traffic was picking up with morning commuters, but Justin flipped on his siren and careened around cars and trucks, knowing every minute counted.

This case was about to blow up in their faces. The crime scene was probably already contaminated six ways till Sunday. And now the suspect pool would only mount.

Not to mention the press...

He saw the first media van roll up just as he and Amanda did. He wished he'd had that coffee Donald Reisling had offered.

It was going to be a helluva long day.

Worse, the unsub would probably be watching the circus and gloating, adding up his body count and choosing his next victim.

AMANDA AND JUSTIN met the school's security guard for the school at the front door and were immediately escorted out to the football stadium where the principal and football coach were keeping watch. The students who'd found the body had been sequestered in the gym with the track coach while all other students had been retained in their homerooms.

Principal Blakely looked haggard as he greeted them at the entrance to the stadium and led them over to Kelly's body where it had been staged on the bleachers at the fifty-yard line.

Emotions caught in Amanda's throat when she saw the young woman's matted hair, ashen skin and eyes glazed with the shock of death. Amanda snapped on latex gloves and handed Justin a pair, and he did the same.

"Who found her?" Justin asked.

"Coach Turner came out here with the track team. The team captain, Naomi Carter, spotted her first. She screamed and everyone else came running."

Amanda winced. "Did the students touch anything?"

"I don't think so," the principal said. "Coach said he shouted at them to stay back. Some of the kids are pretty shaken up."

"Get the counselors with them right away."

"Already done." Blakely shook his head sadly. "I don't understand why a killer would leave her at school."

"To send a message," Justin said.

"There's a string of young women who've gone missing the past ten years from this area," Amanda filled in. "We think their disappearances are related to a former student from Canyon High."

Amanda stooped down to examine Kelly's neck and saw the telltale markings indicating strangulation. Wide marks reddened her throat, marks that looked as if they'd been made by a belt.

"Do these look like the marks on Tina's throat?" she asked.

Justin stooped down to examine them. "Yes. Looks like the same belt was used."

She snapped several photographs with her camera phone while Justin focused on the surrounding area, the bleachers beside the body and the ground beneath her.

Kelly's skirt and blouse were wrinkled, one sleeve torn, but at least her clothing was intact, and she saw no evidence of sexual assault. The ME would have to confirm that though.

"Did you check her hand?" Justin asked.

A bevy of voices sounded behind them, and Amanda realized the ME and backup officers had arrived.

"Get the officers set up to interview the students,"

Justin told the principal. "We'll need all their phones to look at pictures and contacts they've had since then."

"You think one of them killed her?" Blakely asked.

"No," Amanda answered. "But they may have caught some important detail on their cameras that could help us."

The principal headed over to meet the county police and ME and to do as they asked.

Amanda glanced at Kelly's hands. Her left hand was splayed open, her nails jagged as if she'd fought for her life. Hope budded. If she'd fought with her attacker, maybe they'd find the suspect's DNA beneath her fingernails.

Gently, she stroked Kelly's right hand, the one folded up. It was stiff, rigor having set in. "I'm so sorry, Kelly. I wish I'd found you before this happened. But I promise you, I'll catch whoever did this and make them pay."

She uncurled Kelly's fingers, her suspicions confirmed. A class ring was clutched in her palm.

"Same MO," Justin said.

Amanda snapped a picture of it, then lifted the ring, knowing immediately it wasn't Kelly's but had belonged to a boy.

She turned it over and peered at the inside of the band for the engraving. TS. This was Terry's ring.

How had the killer gotten it? And why put it in Kelly's hand?

Had Terry done so as a message that Kelly had always been his?

She bagged it for evidence, hoping they would get something useful from it.

The crime scene team approached, Lieutenant Gibbons in charge. "What did you find?"

Amanda showed him the ring. "A class ring was found in Tina Grimes's hand that had DNA from a previous missing victim. This ring belonged to Terry Sumter, Kelly Lambert's former boyfriend."

"Did she keep it all these years, or did someone plant it in her hand to turn suspicion toward Terry?" Justin said, speculating aloud.

A ruckus sounded near the fence to the stadium, and Amanda saw a media frenzy pushing at the gate, cameras flashing as reporters volleyed for footage.

The sound of more cars roaring up rumbled from the parking lot, then more shouts and voices.

Principal Blakely strode toward them, visibly upset. "Good grief. The word spread and parents are starting to storm the school."

"Get officers out there to control the crowd," Amanda said. The crime scene techs went to work examining the bleachers and football field while Dr. Sagebrush approached the body.

The ME looked reverent as he knelt beside Kelly. "So sad to see someone in their prime taken this way."

And so needless, Amanda thought. But she bit

back the words. Her emotions were teetering close to the surface.

So she stepped aside to let him do his work while she phoned her deputy. She quickly explained what had happened and asked him to bring Sumter to the sheriff's office for questioning.

Suddenly, shouts erupted and she looked up to see Mr. Lambert scaling the fence and running toward them.

"Oh, my God," Amanda whispered.

A deputy was trying to catch him, but Amanda threw up a hand to warn him that it was okay. Not that it really was okay, but the last thing she wanted was the officer pulling a gun on the victim's father and the situation spiraling out of control.

"I've got it," she told the officer.

She rushed toward Mr. Lambert, blocking his view. "Mr. Lambert, I told you to wait and I'd call you."

"I have to see her," he cried. "It's my little girl…."

"I know, and I'm so sorry," Amanda said softly.

She pulled him into a hug and let him sob on her shoulder, her own chest aching with grief and guilt.

JUSTIN DIDN'T DO emotional scenes and had to admit that Amanda was handling it well. Although he noticed the slight shiver in her body. The man's outburst was definitely weighing on her.

Sympathy for her registered. She knew the victim personally and felt responsible because she was the local sheriff. Everyone was looking up to her, counting on her.

She probably viewed today as a failure.

But she'd inherited this mess and he'd make sure she knew it wasn't her fault.

She coaxed Lambert back near the gate, and Justin watched as the ME examined the body.

"The MO consistent with Tina?" Justin asked.

"Belt marks look the same width." The doctor peered at him over the rim of his glasses. "But your killer didn't keep Kelly long."

"He's escalating, wants to show off, taunt us with the fact that he hasn't gotten caught and that he'll keep killing until we stop him."

Shouts near the gate made him jerk his head up, and he saw Lambert still arguing with Amanda, so he strode toward them. Someone had to defuse the situation. The media were taking pictures left and right.

"Mr. Lambert, I'm really sorry for your loss," Justin said as he coaxed him beneath the awning of the snack stand. "But right now you need to go home. Call a friend or family member to stay with you. Someone who can offer you comfort while we investigate."

Lambert's anguished look turned to anger that he directed toward Amanda. "You said you'd find her. I came to you for help and look what happened."

Amanda's hurt look tore at Justin. He understood about grief and anger, but Amanda didn't deserve this.

"Mr. Lambert," he said, his voice turning to steel. "Sheriff Blair did everything in her power to find your daughter, but Kelly's disappearance is related to a string of missing-persons cases that has spanned a decade. She has already made more strides in this investigation than your former sheriff."

Amanda gently took Mr. Lambert's arm. "Please go home, Mr. Lambert. I swear that I'll find the person who did this and lock him up."

She gestured toward the officer who'd been chasing Lambert earlier, and he escorted Lambert toward the exit. Justin saw the feeding frenzy of reporters and parents converging and silently cursed.

But another deputy stepped up to intervene and push them back so he headed over to the principal, who was talking with one of the crime techs.

"Excuse me, Mr. Blakely," Justin said. "Are there security cameras outside the school?"

The principal nodded, although his mouth thinned into a grim line. "We have a few, but not as many as we should, and I think a couple are broken."

Unbelievable with all the school shootings these days. "I want to look at all the feed of the parking lot and area by the stadium for the last twenty-four hours."

Justin gestured toward the crowd in the parking lot. "It's possible that our killer is in that crowd right now watching the commotion. He'll get off on our reactions and the drama."

Because he enjoyed inflicting pain and suffering on the town.

THE VIDEO FEED was all set up so Suzy Turner could watch the commotion. The reporters running to the school for the story. The students in upheaval.

The parents worried and racing to protect their spoiled offspring from the ugliness of the world.

Except they were hypocrites.

Those same parents allowed their teenagers to bully others. To taunt the weaker and berate the less intelligent and to shun the less attractive as if they were lepers.

Suzy Turner was one of them.

When the cameras finally showed Kelly Lambert's dead body sprawled on the bleachers, Suzy would know what her future held.

Not parties and bragging about her looks and money to her classmates.

Oh, she thought she was popular and that everyone loved her.

But they were a fickle lot. They'd quickly forget her just like they'd forgotten the others.

## Chapter Twelve

Amanda and Justin approached the local news reporter, deciding they needed to gain control before the press made things worse. Parents and families were becoming increasingly agitated.

Amanda stepped up on one of the platforms on the outer edge of the stadium. "Folks, I need everyone to listen."

Angry voices shouted at her.

"Was there a teenager killed here this morning?"

"Who was murdered?"

"Why won't you tell us anything?"

"Are there shooters in the school?"

Amanda waved her hand. "Please listen. There was no school shooting, and no students at the school have been injured. Nor do we believe they're in danger."

"Then why is the school on lockdown?"

"A body was found!"

Amanda's hand shot up again. "This morning when the staff and students arrived, they did find the body of a young woman. She has been identified as twenty-seven-year-old Kelly Lambert, who was reported missing two days ago. Miss Lambert was not killed on the school grounds, but rather whoever murdered her left her body on the bleachers."

"Why leave it at the school?"

"Do you think one of the students is responsible?"

"Is the killer in there with our kids?"

Amanda shook her head. "We do not believe any current student at Canyon High is responsible or that the killer is inside the school. However, some students did see the body and we're keeping everyone contained until we can investigate. Your children are only being questioned in case they saw something pertinent to the case, and only with adult counselor supervision." She forced a calm firmness to her voice. "Now, I urge you to go home and go about your day. I promise you the students are safe and sound."

"What if you're wrong and the killer is in the school?" someone shouted.

Amanda tensed. What if she was wrong? No…the killer/kidnapper was now targeting women in their twenties, not teenagers. "Again, we do not think that is the case. Kelly Lambert was left here sometime during the night. The killer was long gone before the students and staff arrived."

But even as she tried to reassure the crowd of restless concerned parents, she wondered if that was true. She didn't think the killer was inside, but what if he'd waited around to see them find Kelly's body?

Justin's gaze scanned the group as Amanda addressed them. Some asinine reporter had been talking to parents and onlookers, stirring up suspicion and panic by asking questions that were off base.

Everyone was restless and imagining the worst, but hopefully Amanda's reassurances would calm them. He saw doubt on many faces though, as if they weren't convinced she was telling the truth.

Principal Blakely took the microphone next, also urging parents to go home. "Folks, we have policies in place for situations like this, and we need your help. As Sheriff Blair stated, your kids are not in danger. If, however, any one of them suffers emotional duress as a result of today's events, we will be offering counseling services.

"Classes are resuming as normal, although sports activities and practices will be cancelled for the day. Buses will run on schedule, as well. Rest assured that if anything changes we will contact you."

He stepped down and began to move through the crowd, personally shaking hands and chatting with individuals until some of the panic settled and individuals began to disperse.

Justin studied the group, his senses honed for anyone who looked overtly nervous, someone filming the pandemonium, someone on the run.

"You did a good job," he told Amanda as they wove past a set of older folks, probably grandparents of some students. The small cluster looked worriedly at Amanda, then bowed their heads in whispers and finally clung to each other as they walked toward the exit.

Justin took Amanda's elbow. "Let's study the footage from the security cameras. Maybe something will stick out."

They walked together to the school guard, who escorted them to the security station inside and showed them the surveillance cameras. One camera was situated on each of the corners of the building with two more covering the gym and football stadium. The emergency exits also had cameras, but the angles were poor.

Unfortunately two of the cameras overlooking the entry points to the stadium had been broken.

Probably by teen pranks, the security guard said. They had been out for six weeks. The principal was waiting on budget approval to have them repaired.

But after surveying the films of the night, they found nothing. No one dragging a body into the stadium. Meaning the killer knew where the broken cameras were.

They moved on to look at the feed of the media and crowd gathered outside.

"What do you see?" Justin asked.

Amanda rubbed her temple. "A town full of concerned parents. I can't blame them. If my child was inside the school and I didn't know what was going on, I'd be anxious, too."

Justin covered her hand with his. An innocent

gesture of camaraderie but one that made him want more. "We will find out who did this."

"I still think we should warn the classmates returning for the reunion."

"Then we'd tip our hand," Justin reasoned. "Right now the perp has no idea we're on to him."

"But that's just it. We're not," Amanda said, her voice riddled with frustration.

Justin squeezed her hand. "Yes, we are. We know he has a reason for targeting your female classmates. Reisling's father looks good for the crimes. And he has enough money to pay someone to alibi him if needed." He drummed his knuckles on the table as he searched the feed. "Do you see Reisling or his father in the crowd?"

Amanda leaned closer, searching. "No."

"Anyone else look out of place?"

"I know a few of the folks but not all of them," she said. "Wait, there's Suzy Turner's mother."

"Who's Suzy Turner?"

"Another classmate," Amanda said. "She looks upset. And she's talking to the principal."

Amanda's phone buzzed, and she snatched it up. "Sheriff Blair."

"It's Principal Blakely. Mrs. Turner is here and says she has to talk to you."

"I'll be right out," Amanda said. She disconnected, then turned to Justin. "Keep looking at the feed. Let me go talk to Mrs. Turner."

He nodded, but a bad premonition hit him. Kelly Lambert had been taken two days ago. And now she was dead.

And Mrs. Turner looked panicked.

Had the unsub taken another victim?

AMANDA RUSHED THROUGH the hallway and outside to the roped-off area around the bleachers, her heart hammering as Suzy Turner's mother rushed toward her. "Amanda," the woman cried. "I'm scared. I can't find Suzy anywhere. I think she's missing." She glanced at the crime scene tape. "When I heard a body was found here, I was terrified it was her."

Amanda's chest constricted. "No, now tell me what happened, Mrs. Turner. Why do you think Suzy is missing?"

"Because she was supposed to come to our house for dinner last night," Mrs. Turner said. "She always comes on Thursday nights. Ever since her father got sick, she never misses a week."

"I'm sorry, I didn't know your husband was ill," Amanda said.

Tears glittered in the woman's eyes. "He has Alzheimer's. Early onset. Suzy didn't like to talk about it, but she knew her time with him was limited, so she wanted to see him while he still remembered her." Her voice broke on the last few words. "You have to find her. I can't lose her, too…."

Amanda squeezed Mrs. Turner's hands. "When was the last time you saw or spoke to her?"

"Yesterday morning. She called and said she'd pick up dessert for that evening. Then she…didn't show."

"Did she tell you what her plans were for the day?"

"Just that she had errands to run. She was in charge of decorations for the reunion." Mrs. Turner rubbed her hands as if to ward off a chill. "I called and called her all night, but there was no answer. So I went to her condo this morning to check on her, but nobody was there."

"What about her car?"

"It was gone."

"Doesn't she travel for her job?" Amanda asked. She faintly remembered that Suzy was in pharmaceutical sales.

"She does travel, but she cancelled work trips until after the reunion."

Everything pointed back to the reunion.

If Amanda didn't call it off soon, there wouldn't be any females left to attend. The unsub had killed Kelly in two days, meaning Suzy's life was in terrible danger.

"I'll need to search her condo, her phones, computer. Maybe something in there can tell us where she went. Hopefully she just had an emergency business meeting."

"I hope so, but it's not like her not to call." Mrs. Turner wiped tears from her eyes. "Do you think the person who killed Kelly has my Suzy?"

Unfortunately she did, but she refused to panic the woman. "We can't jump to that conclusion. Was Suzy upset with anyone, or was she having problems at work or home?"

"No," Mrs. Turner said. "Her job was going great. She just got a promotion."

"How about problems with coworkers?"

"Not that she mentioned."

"Did she have a boyfriend?"

"No one serious. She said there was someone at work, but she wouldn't tell me who he was."

Which made Amanda wonder if he was married. "I'll get over to Suzy's and look around as soon as possible. Do you happen to have a key to her place?"

The woman fidgeted, then pulled one from her purse and gave her the address. "Here, I water her plants when she's out of town." She pushed the key into Amanda's hand. "I can't lose her, Amanda. You have to find her before she ends up like Kelly."

"I promise I'll do everything I can." Of course she'd made the same promise to Kelly Lambert's father and fiancé and she'd failed.

Amanda had to ask one more question. "Did Suzy have trouble with anyone from our class?"

"No," Mrs. Turner said. "Why would you ask that?"

"Just routine questions, ma'am."

"You remember Suzy. She was popular in school, head cheerleader, class vice president and all. Everyone loved her."

Except for the not-so-popular girls who'd been jealous of her. But were any of them jealous enough to hurt her? And after ten years?

That seemed extreme.

"Mrs. Turner, do you remember Donald Reisling and his accident?"

"Of course, that was awful. I felt so sorry for his father, the way Donald shamed him and all."

Hadn't she heard that Lynn had really been driving? Of course, no one had ever proved that....

"Did Suzy date Donald?"

"No...I mean she was nice to him after the accident, tried to be a friend. But I think he wanted more and that would never have worked." Mrs. Turner's eye twitched. "Why? What does Donald have to do with Suzy?"

"I don't know, maybe nothing," Amanda asked.

Still, if she'd rejected Donald, either he or his father might have wanted revenge.


JUSTIN CONTINUED STUDYING the camera feed, his instincts kicking in as he noticed a young man, late twenties to early thirties, with sandy hair and a goatee.

He looked nervous, his gaze shifting back and forth between the spectators as if he was searching for someone. He pushed his way to the front until he reached the edge of the football field and peered over the fence.

One of the officers in charge of clearing the parking lot motioned for people to head back to their cars, and the guy pulled a ball cap lower on his head, jammed his hands in the pockets of his jeans and hurried away.

Justin searched the other cameras to see which vehicle the man went to, but lost him when he faded into an area where the cameras had been broken.

Who was the man and what had he been nervous about?

SUZY TURNER HAD struggled and fought for her life, but to no avail. Now she lay like a limp rag doll, her white blond hair tangled around her face, those sparkling green eyes blank of the normally coy smile that lit them up.

It had been fun to watch her die.

The pictures of the others lined the wall. Julie Kane. Lynn Faust.

Then the final one—Amanda Blair.

Killing her would make the revenge complete.

## Chapter Thirteen

Amanda hurried back to the security station to talk to Justin. He waved her in, his brows furrowed. "I've narrowed the window of time when the body was dumped," Justin said. "Sometime after two a.m." He pointed to one of the cameras near the left entryway to the field. "One of the cameras had been out, but that one was working. Someone shot it out around two-fifteen."

"That could be helpful," Amanda said. "The crime scene team should search for the bullet casing."

"I'll let them know. There's something else I want you to look at."

Amanda eased up beside him. "Okay, but we've got another problem. Mrs. Turner is worried, Justin. She thinks her daughter, Suzy, has disappeared."

Justin cursed. "All right, look at this, then we'll talk about the Turner case." He rewound the camera and zeroed in on the young man with the hat. "Do you recognize him?"

Amanda narrowed her eyes. "Yes, that's Carlton Butts's brother, Ted."

"Did they have a younger sibling at Canyon High?"

She shook her head no.

"Then what's he doing here?"

"I don't know," Amanda admitted. "Maybe he heard about the body and was just curious like half the town."

"Could be. But he looks awfully nervous."

"He does, doesn't he?" Amanda tried to recall the last time she'd seen Ted, but couldn't.

"You said he and his brother weren't close?"

"No, they were too different," Amanda said. "At Carlton's funeral, he told me that he didn't understand Carlton. Ted knew his brother was depressed and had been picked on by the other kids, but he said Carlton brought some of the antagonism on himself."

"So he wouldn't want revenge against the girls who refused to date his brother?"

"I don't think so," Amanda said "But we can talk to him if you want."

Justin said, "We need to look at Suzy's life, her schedule, figure out her movements the day she went missing. Maybe we'll find something to link her disappearance to Kelly's."

She hoped so. The bodies were piling up way too quickly.

Together they walked outside, then drove back to the police station, the gray clouds adding to the gloom mounting inside her.

Terry Sumter sat by the front desk, looking belligerent as they entered the station.

In another chair Mr. Reisling sat beside another man she assumed was his attorney. Reisling looked confident, almost smug.

"Deputy, please escort Mr. Reisling and his lawyer to my office," Justin said. "I'll interview them while the sheriff talks to Mr. Sumter."

Amanda nodded, knowing the interrogations would go quicker if they split up. They'd spent most of the day at the school. Afternoon was fading into early evening and they needed answers.

Needed to find Suzy before it was too late.

Terry glared at her with hate-filled eyes. "You aren't really going to arrest me, are you?"

"Where were you two nights ago?" Amanda asked.

He crossed his feet at the ankles. "You mean the night Kelly disappeared?"

"Yes."

"On a work detail," Sumter said.

Amanda raised a brow. "I thought you lost your job."

"My company fell apart when the building business hit bottom," he said. "But I do some renovations with Harvey Mabry. Two nights ago I was laying floors in Cedartown. Call Harvey and ask him."

"I will." Amanda shoved a notepad in front of Terry. "Write down his contact information."

Terry's hand shook as he took the pen.

"Nervous, Terry? You hiding something?"

His eyes pierced her again. "I just need a drink, that's all."

So he was an alcoholic. "They have AA meetings at the Methodist church."

He dropped his head with a grunt that said he didn't appreciate her advice, scribbled the number, then handed it to her.

"Terry, have you seen Suzy Turner lately?"

"No, she left a message on my machine about the reunion, but I didn't call her back. No one there I want to see."

"Stay put while I call Harvey." She stepped aside and punched the man's number, then explained that she needed to know if Terry was working the night Kelly disappeared.

"Yeah, he was with my crew all day and half the night laying floors. Didn't get done till after four a.m. Terry's not a bad guy when he leaves the booze alone."

She wondered if that was why his business had failed instead of the economy.

She thanked him, then hung up. "Terry, do you still have your class ring?"

"No, I gave it to Lynn years ago. When we broke up, I didn't want it back." He flexed his hands, looked at his empty ring finger. "Why are you asking about my class ring?"

Amanda gritted her teeth. "I can't say at this point."

But if Terry had given Lynn his class ring, how had it ended up in Kelly Lambert's hand?

JUSTIN STUDIED REISLING. Interrogating him again would probably be a waste of time. The man had money and power and wielded it like a sword.

But he was the most viable suspect they had.

"First of all, let me introduce myself," the astute gray-haired man in the three-piece suit said. "I'm Mr. Reisling's attorney, Jay Edward Fuller."

Justin tapped his badge. "Sergeant Thorpe, Texas Ranger. And before you start throwing up a bunch of legal jargon, I want you to know why we asked Mr. Reisling to come in."

"He explained that you're investigating a missing woman named Kelly Lambert."

"Actually she's no longer missing, as I'm sure you're aware if you've seen the news today. Her body was found at the high school this morning. So now we're dealing with a homicide."

Mr. Reisling averted his eyes. "Such a shame. She was such a nice young woman."

Justin's brow shot up at Reisling's sarcastic tone. "I understand that you disliked her because she didn't want anything to do with your son after the accident that paralyzed him. At least that was my earlier impression."

"All those snotty kids did abandon him," Reisling shot back.

"Don't say anything else," Fuller warned in a low tone.

Justin's mouth twitched as he fought a smile. He

enjoyed seeing the jerk put in his place. And if he was the killer, he wanted to see him rot in jail.

"Where were you two nights ago?" Justin asked.

Reisling smoothed down his tie. "In Austin on business."

"You have someone who can verify that?"

Reisling glanced at his attorney and his attorney gave a clipped nod. "I met with a client. And yes, she'll alibi me."

Justin propped himself on the edge of the desk, folded his arms and leaned forward, scrutinizing him. "What about last night?"

Reisling fidgeted and looked at his lawyer for guidance. Fuller's expression was a complete blank. The man had a great poker face.

"What time?" Fuller asked.

"Between two-fifteen and six-thirty," Justin said. "That's when the guard comes on duty at the school."

Reisling's lips compressed into a thin, straight line. "I was home in bed like everyone else in this godforsaken town."

"Not everyone," Justin said. "Someone was dropping off Kelly Lambert's body so the teenagers at school would find her this morning."

Reisling scowled and started to say something, but Fuller placed a hand on the other man's arm and shook his head. "We came in as a courtesy, Sergeant Thorpe, but I've heard enough. Unless you're going to arrest my client, we're done here." Fuller stood and Reisling followed.

Irritated, Justin worked his jaw from side to side. "Mr. Reisling, do you know Suzy Turner?"

Hatred flashed in the man's eyes for a millisecond before he disguised it with a phony smile. "Of course. She went to school with my son."

"What's going on?" Fuller asked.

"We believe Kelly Lambert's murder is related to a string of other disappearances from this area and counties across the state. The common link is the high school, more specifically the girls who attended school with Mr. Reisling's son."

Awareness dawned in the lawyer's eyes, and Justin realized that Reisling hadn't filled his attorney in on his son's background. Fuller must not be from Sunset Mesa or he'd already know.

"You're looking for a serial kidnapper/killer?" Fuller asked.

Justin nodded. "And your client had motive to hurt each of the missing girls."

"How DID IT go with Reisling?" Amanda asked as she drove to Carlton Butts's mother's house. She wasn't sure if his brother still lived there, but since Mrs. Butts relied on a walker and had trouble getting around, she took a chance that the woman didn't live alone.

The home was located in a low-rent section of town that kids used to call the poor houses, another reason Carlton had literally been the butt of other kids' taunts. Ten years had intensified the weathered paint and rotting boards, proving no one, real-estate developer or individual, had decided to keep up the properties. Dark clouds shrouded the sky, adding an eerie look to the area. Weeds and dead flowers choked the yards, trees that had blown down in a storm still hadn't been cut and hauled away and the vehicles parked in the drives confirmed that the owners were low-income families barely able to survive.

Too bad Terry Sumter hadn't taken it upon himself to upgrade this property. He could probably pick up the houses for a song and flip them, then turn his life around.

But he was not Amanda's problem. Unless he'd killed Kelly and Tina and kidnapped the other victims.

She parked and cut the engine. "I used to come out here to work on science projects with Carlton. I still can't believe he committed suicide."

"Did his mother see the signs?"

"I don't know," Amanda said as they walked up the cement driveway.

She rang the doorbell, but it wasn't working, so Justin knocked. He was studying the property and woods behind it as if he expected trouble.

Footsteps shuffled inside, and the sound of a key being turned echoed through the door. Finally, Mrs.

Butts cracked the door open and peered out, but she was leaning heavily on her walker.

"Mrs. Butts," Amanda said. "It's Amanda Blair, Sheriff Blair now." She gestured toward Justin. "This is Sergeant Thorpe with the Texas Rangers. We'd like to talk to you and your son."

"My son is dead," she said bitterly.

Amanda detected the strong scent of whiskey on her breath and realized Carlton's mother must, like Terry, have a problem with booze. Her once-brown hair had gray stripes and was uncombed, and she tugged a ratty bathrobe tighter around her neck as if they'd just woken her.

"I know Carlton died," she said, wondering if the woman simply wanted to make a point or if she was senile. "But we'd like to talk to your other son Ted."

Mrs. Butts put more weight on her walker. "What about?"

"Is Ted here, ma'am?" Justin asked.

"Why would he be? He don't live here anymore."

"Where does he live?" Amanda asked.

"Other side of town. Got one of those cabins near the creek."

Tina Grimes's body had been found in Camden Creek.

"Is that where he'd be now?" Amanda asked.

"Naw, he should be at work. What you want with Ted?"

"He was at the high school earlier when Kelly Lambert's body was found."

Mrs. Butts's eyes widened, tinged with fear. "I'm sure a lot of other folks were there, too."

"Most of them were parents of students in the school," Amanda pointed out.

Justin gripped the edge of the door. "Where does your son work?"

"He owns a cabinet shop. Does custom work for those big fancy developments going up in the neighboring counties."

"Has he kept up with any of his former classmates from school?" Amanda asked.

Mrs. Butts shook her head. "No, why would he? After the way they treated Carlton, he decided they weren't worth his time."

"So he was still mad at people over Carlton's death?" Justin asked.

The woman's eyes darted back and forth between them as if she suddenly realized she'd said too much. "Ted's a good boy," she said defensively. "He went to college and got a degree in business. Manages his own shop." She wagged her finger at Amanda. "Don't you dare turn on him like you did Carlton."

Guilt suffused Amanda. She hadn't turned on Carlton. But she also hadn't remained close friends. She'd been caught up in her own life. "Is Ted going to the reunion?" Amanda asked.

"You'll have to ask him," Mrs. Butts said. "Although he may want to show those little twits that he made something of himself."

Amanda thanked the woman; then she and Justin walked back to the car.

Mrs. Butts's comment about her turning on Carlton gnawed at her. If she'd stayed closer to Carlton, could she have saved him from committing suicide?

Ten minutes later, they stood inside Ted's cabinet shop. Amanda was impressed with the details of his carpentry work and understood why he'd landed projects with the developers building high-end estate homes.

She spoke to the receptionist, a redhead with streaks of black in her hair and red cowboy boots. "Howdy. What can we do for you?"

Amanda and Justin both identified themselves. "Can we talk to Ted?"

"Let me check and see if he's busy with a customer." She rose, teetering on her high-heeled boots, and disappeared through a doorway. The sound of voices echoed from the back; then she reappeared and led them through a set of double doors to an office that surprised Amanda with its modern design.

"Hello, Amanda," Ted said.

Gone was the ball cap from the camera feed. His hair was close cropped, his button-down shirt and jeans giving him a professional but casual look. He'd aged some since she'd seen him, but there was such a stark difference between him and Carlton that she understood how Carlton had felt like the underdog in comparison.

"It looks like your business is doing well," Amanda said.

He shrugged, but his eyes glittered with pride. "Yeah, I like my business." He glanced at Justin. "But you two didn't come to talk to me about my cabinets, did you?"

Amanda shifted. "Why were you outside the school today?"

Unease flickered in his eyes. "I heard the news and was curious like everyone else, I guess."

"Did you keep up with Kelly?" Justin asked.

He shook his head. "She called about the reunion and left a message. I never called her back."

"Are you going to attend?" Amanda asked.

He smoothed a hand over a wood sample. "Not sure yet. It's not like I kept close friends with anyone there. After Carlton died, it was…hard."

"What about Suzy Turner?" Justin asked. "Have you seen her lately?"

"Suzy?" His voice cracked. "Don't tell me she's missing, too."

"Her mother thinks so," Amanda said.

"Answer the question," Justin asked. "Have you seen her lately?"

"No. But she left a message about the reunion, too. Said she was bringing a new boyfriend. You know she always liked to brag about herself."

"Did you have a thing for her?" Justin asked.

"You've got to be kidding. Snotty girls aren't my type." His eyes flashed with annoyance; then a mask slid over his face. "Listen, Amanda, I didn't hang out with those girls in school, and it's been ten years since Carlton died. If you think I've held some grudge against them, you're wrong." He rubbed a finger along one of the ridges of a cabinet. "I loved my brother, but I told him he needed to grow thicker skin. Then he killed himself and I had to pick up the pieces of my mom." Anger hardened his voice. "I don't blame the kids at school. I blame Carlton. He took the coward's way out and destroyed our family in the process."

"WELL, THAT WAS a surprise," Justin said as they left the cabinet shop. "Ted had good reason to harbor a grudge against the girls who ridiculed his brother, but he doesn't seem to."

"I told you I didn't think they got along," Amanda said. "He's obviously still angry with Carlton for killing himself."

"He's right, that is the coward's way out," Justin said. "But since he doesn't seem to hold a grudge, he doesn't seem like a likely suspect."

Amanda punched in Mrs. Turner's number, hoping for a miracle—that Suzy had shown up by now. The woman answered on the second ring, her voice raspy as if she'd been crying. "Hello, Amanda."

"Have you heard from Suzy?"

"No, did you find her?"

Amanda winced at the desperate hope in the

woman's voice. "Not yet. I'm on my way to her place right now to look around."

"Do you need me to come over?"

"No, just let me know if you hear from her." Amanda hung up and swung the vehicle onto the main road leading to the condos. Night had fallen, the land bathed in darkness as she left town and sped down the road.

Suddenly a dark car shot out of a side street, raced up behind her and started around her. Irritated, she flipped on the siren, but the car simply sped up instead of falling back or pulling over.

The windows were tinted so dark she couldn't see inside, but the window slid down a fraction of an inch and suddenly a gunshot blasted the air.

Amanda ducked, swerving right as the bullet shattered the driver's window. Glass sprayed her and a burning sensation shot through her left arm.

Justin cursed and grabbed the steering wheel as the squad car spun out of control and slid toward the ravine.

## Chapter Fourteen

Justin jerked his gun from his holster, hoping to get off a round at the shooter, but Amanda had been hit, and the car was out of control.

"I've got the wheel," Amanda said, struggling to right the car and keep it from crashing.

He swung his gun up behind her head and fired, but the dark sedan surged forward, its taillights disappearing into the night. His breath rasped out as he squinted to read the license plate, but the car had no tag.

The squad car slammed into the bank to the right, then spun sideways and screeched to a stop. He jerked forward, but the seat belt caught him, and Amanda gripped the steering wheel. He expected the air bags to pelt them, but the impact must not have been strong enough to trigger them.

"Dammit, he got away!" Amanda shouted.

Justin's heart hammered. "Where are you hit?"

"My arm, but it's just a flesh wound." Amanda shoved hair from her face. "Did you see the shooter?"

"No, did you?"

She shook her head. "The windows were too dark."

"There was no license plate either," Justin said.

"It was a planned attack." Amanda closed her eyes and leaned back against the seat, and Justin wondered if she'd lied about the seriousness of her injury. Flesh wounds still stung like the devil and now her adrenaline was wearing off, she might be feeling the pain.

"Let me see your arm," he said, forcing his voice to be gentle when he wanted to tear after that car and beat the hell out of the SOB who'd shot her.

Amanda sighed, twisting around to look at him. "I'm fine. But obviously the killer wants to stop us from asking questions."

He pulled her hand toward him. "Let me see, Amanda."

Emotions swirled in the depths of her eyes. It had been a hell of a day and she looked exhausted.

"I should have stopped this guy before now," she murmured.

Guilt deepened her voice, making his heart tug. Kelly Lambert's father had blamed her for not finding his daughter in time. Mrs. Butts blamed her for abandoning her son.

Amanda blamed herself for another classmate's disappearance.

It wasn't right.

Unable to stop himself, he pulled her into his arms. "None of this is your fault, Amanda. You're doing a great job."

She shook her head, her hair brushing his chin, but she didn't pull away. "But I promised Mr. Lambert I'd find Kelly, and now Suzy is missing."

Justin stroked her back, soothing her. "I've worked cases like this before. The killer seems like he's one step ahead, but eventually he screws up. We will find him, Amanda."

He felt Amanda's soft breath on his neck as she lifted her head to look up at him. "But it's not enough. If I don't make an arrest soon, Suzy might end up like Kelly."

Justin bit his tongue to keep from telling her that if the unsub had Suzy, she was probably already dead. Since there was no sign of sexual assault, it was clear the motive was murder.

Only the suspect had disposed of the bodies where they couldn't be found with the first few cases, but had recently decided to claim the kills.

Because he was ready to send a message and receive the glory for the crimes.

He cradled Amanda's face between his hands. "Listen to me, Amanda. We're law officers. We hunt down the bad guys, but we're still human. We can't save everyone."

"But we have to try," she whispered.

He nodded, his heart hammering. "Yes, and we will get him."

She looked so vulnerable that his eyes were drawn to her mouth. He wanted to kiss her. Hold her.

Promise her everything would be all right.

His lips touched hers. Soft. Gentle. Hungry.

She parted her lips in invitation, and he deepened the kiss, tracing her mouth with his tongue. She moaned softly and clung to him, her fingers stroking his back.

A heartbeat later, her phone rang and she eased away from him. For a brief second, he felt bereft, as if he'd lost something important.

Only how could he lose something he'd never had?

AMANDA SHIVERED AT the intensity in Justin's expression. Lord help her, she could drown in those sultry bedroom eyes.

He was so strong and in control, so masculine and confident, so protective—exactly like her father had been.

She'd been devastated when she'd lost him.

How would she survive if she allowed herself to fall for Justin and something happened to him?

He could have been killed a minute ago.

*So could you, and you would never have known what it was like to be in his arms. To feel his kiss.*

Her phone buzzed like a siren again, and she jolted back to reality. Good grief, she was supposed to be working.

She snatched up the phone. "Sheriff Blair."

"It's Deputy Morgan. I wanted to let you know I looked at the list of people Lambert turned down for loans. Two of them have moved on. The other is old man Gentry. He's almost ninety so I don't see him kidnapping or killing anyone."

"Thanks for checking it out, Deputy."

She disconnected and reached for the keys, but Justin caught her hands.

"Let me look at that arm first."

Her arm was stinging, and he would persist unless she proved that she was okay. The bullet had grazed the upper part of her shoulder so she had to undo the top few buttons of her uniform shirt to show him.

Heat blazed in his eyes as he watched her unfasten the buttons. She knew the plain khaki shirt wasn't sexy, but she was still a woman and had donned a lacy black bra beneath it.

His smile of appreciation made her belly flutter with awareness and desire. Her nipples budded, practically begging for him to touch them.

But she leaned sideways so he could examine her arm, ignoring the pull of attraction. The bullet had skimmed the skin, tearing her shirt, and her flesh was red like a burn. But the bullet hadn't lodged inside her arm.

"We need to find that bullet," Justin said.

Amanda nodded, her heart squeezing when he bent his head and placed a kiss on her flesh wound. "We'll treat that with some cream later."

"It's fine," Amanda said, swallowing back the emotions his tenderness stirred. Since when had a man been tender with her?

Most guys thought she was such a tomboy they

didn't bother. Of course that was when she had a rare date. She was more the "friend" type. They treated her as if she was one of the guys.

Unable to stand being so close to him and not touching him or kissing him again, she hurriedly fastened her blouse while he searched the floor for the bullet casing. Several seconds later, he plucked it from the door on his side.

He used a penlight to examine it. "Looks like a .38. I'll send it to the lab for analysis."

Amanda focused back on the case, then pulled onto the highway before she did something insane like throw herself at him.

JUSTIN SILENTLY CURSED himself as Amanda drove toward the Turner place. What the hell was wrong with him?

He never allowed himself to become involved with a suspect or a law enforcement officer. He normally liked sexy women who wanted a romp in the sack with no baggage, no ties, no commitments.

No expectations.

Amanda fit none of those requirements.

Well, maybe she fit one. She didn't seem as if she was looking to settle down. She was just as career focused as him. Growing up under the thumb of a Ranger, she obviously wanted to follow in his footsteps.

But her job could get her killed.

Protective instincts that had reared their ugly head

at him when that bullet zinged through the window fought their way to the surface again.

Dammit, he shouldn't care. She was just another coworker.

*Except she might be a target of this nutcase.*

"Did Donald Reisling ever ask you out?" Justin asked.

Amanda slanted him an odd look. "Why would you ask that?"

"Just curious. Did he?"

Amanda's pretty lips formed a pout. Or maybe they simply were plump from his kisses.

Damn, he wanted to plump them up some more.

"No, he was a star athlete," she said, self-deprecation in her voice. "I told you I wasn't in the popular crowd."

"But you're attractive and you were athletic and smart. The guys had to see that."

"We're talking about *teenagers*," Amanda said, emphasizing the last word. "The only thing on their brains was sex. And I wasn't that kind of girl either."

He hadn't expected that she was. Which also made him like her more.

And want her more.

He balled his hands into fists. He had to get a grip.

"So after the accident when the popular girls rejected Reisling, did he seek friendships with you or anyone that he hadn't befriended before?"

Amanda chewed her bottom lip. "No, not that I remember. I heard he fell into a deep depression for a while. And of course, he underwent physical therapy."

"That's understandable."

"Why the questions about Donald?"

"Because someone just shot at us. Rather you," he said. "And Donald Reisling's father is one of our primary suspects."

A frisson of alarm splintered her face. "You think that he might target me?"

Justin hated to voice the thought aloud. But he had to follow the clues and evidence. And if that didn't work, he'd rely on his gut instincts.

Someone had just tried to kill Amanda.

He wanted to find the SOB and lock him up before he finished her off like he had Kelly, Tina and the other victims whose bodies hadn't yet been found.

AMANDA STIFLED THOUGHTS of that heated kiss as she and Justin entered the high-rise condo development. They stopped at the security desk, identified themselves and explained the situation.

One look at Justin's credentials and her badge, and the beefy guy escorted them to the elevator.

"You have surveillance cameras?" Justin asked.

"Yes, sir. If Suzy was abducted, it wasn't from here."

Amanda frowned. Nothing was impossible. But the fact that this building had built-in security points at the front and cameras stationed throughout the hall and elevators would definitely make a kidnapping more difficult.

With Kelly, fake texts had been sent to lure her into a trap. Had the same thing happened to Suzy?

The guard pointed out the camera near the elevator, only three feet from Suzy's door, making Amanda even more sure that the perp hadn't abducted Suzy from her condo.

She inserted the key into the lock, and opened the door. Justin reached out a hand and urged her to stay back.

"Let me check out the interior first."

Even though she doubted the killer was there, Amanda pulled her own gun.

Suzy might be inside the condo.

But she might not be alive.

Suzy Turner could still wear her cheerleading uniform after ten years. All those exercise classes and body-toning treatments and personal trainers had paid off.

Too bad she wouldn't need them anymore now she was dead.

But wouldn't her mother be proud she'd kept her figure?

Her darling, pretty daughter had danced and cheered and teased all the boys ten years ago.

She'd broken dozens of hearts. Trampled on them as if they were ants that needed stomping out at a picnic.

No more.

Now Suzy would lie dead instead of partying with her friends.

The circus at the school had been fun to watch today.

Tomorrow would be even better. Even if they didn't find Suzy tonight, they would find her.

Then another one would die.

## Chapter Fifteen

Justin hesitated at the doorway of the condo, studying the scene. Amanda gasped beside him.

The cushions on the white sofa had been slashed, the stuffing pouring out, something black that looked like ashes smearing the fabric.

Was it symbolic? Was the unsub trying to send a message, or had Suzy's place simply been an opportunity for the perp to vent his rage?

Amanda eased inside, her gun poised to fire, and they swept the living room and kitchen. He gestured that he would search the room off the right side of the hall and she took the left.

One look into the master bedroom, and he realized Suzy was compulsive with organization and design. The condo was a showcase, not a place he'd want to live in. Expensive furniture, artwork, vases, white carpet.

Nothing that felt like home.

No personal photographs or worn tennis shoes or holey jeans. Did the woman really live here, or was it just a stop between travels?

Her closet had been opened, several evening gowns slashed and strewn across the floor. Others had been left hanging, neat and at equal intervals, designer shoes still encased in their original fabric dust bags or boxes.

But no one was inside.

He inched to the master bath, half expecting Suzy's dead body to be lying on the floor or in the bathtub, although he didn't know why. So far, only two of the missing women had been found, both strangled.

Neither in their own homes.

He scanned the bathroom, again noting plush white towels and a glass shelf filled with cosmetics.

Although some bottles had been broken, thrown against the wall, the contents spilled out.

Then he noticed there was water in the garden tub. He stepped closer, leaned over and spotted a corsage floating in it.

Questions ticked in his head.

A class ring had been found in Tina's and Kelly's hand. Rings that signified the class preparing to gather for Canyon High's reunion.

Was this corsage significant? Violets. Were they the same type of flowers she'd worn to homecoming or prom?

AMANDA'S LUNGS STRAINED for a breath as she eased her way through the hall and into Suzy's home office. She'd already noted the destruction of the entertainment system in the living room, but a laptop sat on another desk in the office.

This one hadn't been smashed. Instead it was open, and a screen saver displayed a ten-year-old photograph of Suzy and the cheerleading squad. Suzy's blond hair gleamed beneath the camera lights, her smile boasting no telling how many dollars' worth of dental work.

Amanda's heart began to pound.

Was there a specific reason the intruder had left this computer unharmed? Did the photo of Suzy and the other cheerleaders mean something?

She quickly checked the closet, but it was empty. Relief spilled through her that she hadn't found Suzy's body. Not that it meant Suzy was still alive.

But until they had her body, there was hope.

Amanda noted dozens of fliers and stacks of mail on the chrome desk, one file box designated for work. But most of the other mail pertained to the reunion and the upcoming plans for the celebration.

"The bedroom's clear," Justin said, startling her.

She glanced over her shoulder. "Did you find anything?"

"Her bedroom was trashed like the living room. The bathtub was full of water, and a corsage was floating inside."

Amanda's pulse jumped. "A corsage?"

"A wristband of violets a teenage girl would wear to homecoming or prom."

"Good grief," Amanda said. "Class rings. Corsages. It all keeps coming back to the school."

"And whatever happened ten years ago to tick off the perp."

Perspiration trickled down the back of Amanda's neck. "Look at this." She gestured toward the screen saver. "I doubt even Suzy was still stuck in time enough to keep this on her computer. Especially one she uses for work."

Justin leaned toward the screen, studying the photos. "Who are the girls?"

Amanda swallowed hard and pointed them out from left to right. "Melanie Hoit, Julie Kane, Lynn Faust, Kelly Lambert and Suzy in the front row. Anise Linton, Mona Pratt and Eleanor Goggins in the back row."

"Two of the girls in the front row are dead and now another is missing," Justin surmised.

Worry kicked in Amanda's gut. "I wonder if that means Julie and Lynn are next."

"There's the back row, too," Justin said.

Amanda contemplated what they knew so far. "But Avery Portland, one of the original victims, wasn't a cheerleader. And neither was Tina Grimes, Carly Edgewater, or Denise Newnan. At least not at Canyon High."

"True. But somehow they fit the victimology or knew the unsub."

Amanda glanced up at Justin. "We have to warn the rest of the cheerleaders that they're in danger."

Justin hesitated.

They had already questioned Anise, Mona and Eleanor about Kelly's disappearance. "Let's think about that. We don't want to panic anyone. And with Kelly's death, they're probably already on edge."

Unease prickled Amanda's spine. "What if we're looking at this all wrong? We know Donald Reisling had a reason to hate the women. But what if our killer is a female? A woman from our class who feels like these girls cheated her out of something."

"Like making the cheerleading squad?" Justin asked.

"That does seem thin for a motive, doesn't it?" Amanda said.

Justin shrugged. "Not if the girl has mental problems. Sometimes unstable people zero in on a specific event as the pivotal moment in their life, the event that destroyed their future. The perp could have tried out, failed and been shunned by the ones who did make it. She thinks that if she'd only made the squad, she would have been popular, would have had more friends, success…a different life."

"Then we need to look at the roster and find out who was cut." Amanda felt a burst of adrenaline. "I'll talk to the cheerleading coach. She might have some insight."

"We should speak with the school counselor, too," Justin said. "The counselor would know if a specific student had emotional issues that fit the profile."

"Good idea."

"Have you seen a purse or cell phone?"

"No."

"I'll search for one while you scan her emails." Justin glanced around the condo. "If the unsub didn't take her from here, he might have sent her a text to lure her away like he did Kelly."

Amanda frowned. "But even if he didn't take her from the condo, the suspect was here. We should look at the surveillance tapes and see who came in and out."

"I'll ask the guard to get tapes of the last twenty-four hours for us."

Amanda's pulse pounded. Hopefully they would finally catch a break.

JUSTIN QUICKLY PHONED the guard, filled him in and asked him to pull the tapes. Then he hurriedly searched the office bookcase, various shelves, the hall closet and the bedroom, but found no purse or phone. Another sweep of the den didn't turn up anything either.

Had Suzy left of her own accord to meet someone, then been ambushed?

"I didn't find the phone or purse," he told Amanda. "I'm going to look at those tapes while you finish with her computer."

"Call me if you find anything," Amanda said, her attention on the screen. "I'll see what her schedule looked like before she disappeared."

He rushed into the hallway, and rode the elevator to the main floor and met the guard.

The guard escorted him down the hall into a large room with several screens showing views of the building, hallways and elevator.

"This is from the last twenty-four hours."

Justin slid into one of the chairs and watched as the guard set the tapes for him to review. The guard identified each of the residents as they appeared outside and inside the building, seemed to know the make and model of cars they drove and other tidbits of personal information he'd picked up on the job.

One unit had had furniture delivered the previous day, but the resident had been home to sign for it and let the deliveryman in. UPS delivered several packages along with FedEx. A cleaning service that worked the building came and went, cleaning the common areas, while several of the units had obviously hired them, as well. The residents consisted of young singles or couples in their thirties who worked.

He sat up straighter as Suzy Turner exited her unit at eight a.m. the previous morning. She looked distracted, was checking her phone messages and juggling her briefcase as she rushed toward the elevator.

She'd been very much alive.

He wanted to know what was on her phone.

"What kind of car did Suzy drive?"

"A silver BMW," the guard said. He recited the license plate off the top of his head.

Justin punched his chief's number and requested the tech analyst get copies of Suzy's phone records, then asked him to put an APB on her car.

"I'll get back to you," his chief said.

Justin's mind churned as he scoured through the rest of the tapes. The same cleaning crew that had worked the building entered Suzy's apartment around 1:00 p.m.

Or was it the same crew?

There was only one woman. Her head was wrapped in a scarf like one of the workers from the company, but she was alone.

"Does the crew ever split up on jobs?" he asked.

The guard shrugged. "Sometimes they do for individual cleaning jobs."

He studied the woman again, frowning when he noticed she was wearing a pair of black boots. Hadn't she been wearing tennis shoes earlier?

He rewound the tape and studied the footage, his pulse spiking. Yes, the woman with the scarf had worn tennis shoes in the previous shot.

Why would she change her shoes?

Unless it wasn't the same woman…

Could Amanda be right? Was their unsub a female, maybe a former classmates who held a grudge?

AMANDA MET THE crime team at the door to Suzy's condo and explained the situation. "Any forensics you can find might help stop this guy."

They went straight to work while she finished

combing Suzy's computer files. Suzy was active on social media, but most of her posts pertained to business and her active social life. Apparently she had hit the million-dollar sale mark at work, traveled to Europe constantly, and liked to shop online at expensive boutiques.

Amanda faintly remembered her once saying that she wouldn't be caught dead in a department-store find or in a dress that another girl might own.

Amanda searched for a boyfriend and found several flirtatious notes between her and a man named Syd who lived in London, but nothing definitive. Another flurry of notes discussed the upcoming reunion with Kelly, Julie and Lynn.

She found a photo gallery of old high school candids in a file that had been organized into a slideshow accompanied by music. It seemed to be intended to be shown at the reunion dinner. One shot captured her attention—Suzy in her prom dress standing beside her date.

Amanda immediately zeroed in on the corsage.

Violets, just like the ones floating in Suzy's tub.

She scrolled through the photos again, searching for signs of a classmate who might be jealous of Suzy and the other cheerleaders, but no one stuck out. Most were shots of pep rallies, dances, ball games and couples at parties.

Another photo showed Suzy, Julie Kane and Lynn Faust working the kissing booth at the county fair.

In the background, Amanda spotted Donald in his wheelchair watching from a distance, looking sullen.

A bad premonition tightened Amanda's throat. Julie and Lynn were the next victims. She knew it in her soul.

She checked the latest emails Suzy had received and found one from Julie telling Suzy to meet her at the malt shop where they used to hang out as teens.

Amanda punched Justin's number. "I might have something." She explained about the email.

"Meet me downstairs and we'll go together," Justin said. "If the email was a lure to get both Julie and Suzy at the same time, and they met, maybe we'll find a witness who saw one of them."

Amanda's pulse clamored as she told the head of the crime team where she was going. Justin met her in the lobby, and they rushed outside to the squad car. She started the engine, praying she was wrong, that Julie hadn't been abducted along with Suzy.

LURING SUZY AND Julie to the diner had been brilliant. Neither one had suspected a thing.

Suzy would be appalled to know that everyone would see her looking so pale in death. Normally her makeup was perfect. Now mascara streaked her cheeks and her skin was a pasty yellowish white.

And Julie…ahh, Julie, the prom queen. She had expected to return in full glory, showing off the fact that she'd married her high school lover and accumulated a fortune.

But money and looks hadn't saved them.

Now everyone in town would see them as they should have all along. Silly, ugly girls who gave nothing back to the world. Silly, ugly girls who'd hurt others.

Silly, ugly girls who'd had to die.

## Chapter Sixteen

Images of Suzy and Julie haunted Amanda—images of them dead.

She had to hurry.

"Call information and get Julie's telephone number," she said. "If the unsub doesn't already have her, we need to warn her."

Justin snatched his phone from his pocket and stabbed the number for information while she sped from the condo development and veered onto the highway leading back toward town.

Darkness bathed the rugged landscape between the two towns, worry gnawing at her. Julie's phone rang over and over, but no one answered. Finally the message machine clicked on, and Justin left a voice mail asking Julie to call the sheriff as soon as she received the message.

"I have a bad feeling we're too late," Amanda said.

"No one has reported Julie missing," Justin pointed out, offering her a tiny thread of hope to cling to.

"That doesn't mean she's safe," Amanda said. "Did you find anything on the surveillance tapes?"

"Maybe. There's a cleaning service that works the building. I saw them go in and out of several units. There were three women and a man. Later, I saw a woman go in Suzy's condo who looked suspicious."

"How?"

"She was wearing a scarf like the woman in the cleaning group, but this time she wore black boots instead of tennis shoes."

Amanda jerked her gaze toward him. "You think it was a different woman?"

He nodded. "She might have been the one to trash the place."

"Could you tell who it was?"

"Didn't get a look at her face. She kept it hidden from the cameras," Justin said. "But I asked the guard to courier it to the lab for analysis. Hopefully they can do something to help us identify her."

It was a long shot, but with technology today, they could look at different angles, shadows, reflections, enhance the image…

Amanda took the turn on two wheels, then braked, reminding herself that an accident would only delay the search. But as she wove through town, the fear in the pit of her stomach intensified.

Memories of watching Suzy and Julie cheer flashed back. The class picnic before graduation. The floats for the homecoming parade.

The football win celebrations at the diner.

And the dances at the gym and local party event center. A center Lynn's mother owned and ran.

She squeezed the steering wheel tighter and made the turn into the square, noting that the diner was practically empty tonight, the dinner crowd having thinned out. With people starting to come into town for the reunion, she was surprised there weren't more cars.

If the suspect was following the time line—a countdown—he or she might be planning their end-game for Saturday night.

She had to put an end to this before anyone else in her class died.

JUSTIN'S GUT TOLD him that Suzy was already dead and Julie might be with her. But he refrained from commenting, not wanting to add more pressure on Amanda.

She looked strained and exhausted, and the case wasn't over yet.

She parked in front of the diner, gold and orange lights forming the name, a string of green ones in the shape of a cactus decorating the door. The place looked like a cross between a Mexican cantina and an old-fashioned soda shop, he noted as they entered and he saw the orange vinyl booths and stools at the bar.

"Why would they choose this place to meet?" Justin asked. It certainly didn't look like the martini bar he'd imagined the women frequenting.

"Because this was the old hangout spot in high school," Amanda said. "Teens used to come here after all the ball games. They still do." She pointed to the menu. "No alcohol, but they have the best burgers and milkshakes of any place I've ever been."

His stomach growled. "Maybe we should grab something while we're here." They hadn't bothered to break for lunch.

"You can order us some burgers while I talk to the owner, Max, and his wife."

Justin slid onto a bar stool and picked up a menu. He ordered three burgers and two fries, his gaze scanning the room. An elderly couple sat in a corner booth sharing a chocolate malt. Three middle-aged women had huddled in another one chatting and laughing as they shared coffee and pie.

Teenagers eating burgers and drinking sodas and shakes sat to the left, half of them glued to their cell phones while the others were griping about a school project that was due soon and that nobody had even started yet.

Deciding he'd let Amanda question the owner and waitress, he went to look around. A hall led to the restrooms so he headed that way, but he didn't see anything suspicious. Not that he'd expected to find a body in the hall, but he had considered that the perp might dump Suzy outside.

He noted a back door and pushed at the knob. It swung open to an alley with a Dumpster.

His breath whooshed out in relief. Suzy's body hadn't been left here.

Maybe she was still alive.

AMANDA APPROACHED MARY LOU, Max's wife, where she sat refilling napkin holders at a table near the kitchen.

"Mary Lou, can I talk to you for a minute?"

"Sure, Amanda. I mean, Sheriff." The older woman clucked. "Lordy, I can't get used to seeing you in that uniform. Seems like yesterday you were in here drinking chocolate shakes and doing algebra."

Amanda forced a smile. It seemed like eons ago to her. "I still love those shakes."

Mary Lou smiled. "Your daddy did, too. God rest his soul."

A pang of longing seared Amanda. She still missed her father every day. "I'm sure you heard about Kelly Lambert's death."

Mary Lou closed the napkin holder. "So sad. I can't believe she was murdered and left at the school like that. What kind of person would do such a thing?"

"That's why I'm here, Mary Lou. We believe that Suzy Turner is missing now."

Mary Lou gasped, one hand flying to her chest. "Oh, no. Not Suzy."

Amanda wanted to soothe her, but she couldn't

lie. Not now. Not when they needed everyone in the town's help to find this unsub.

"We searched Suzy's place, and discovered that someone trashed her condo. We also found an email indicating that she was supposed to meet Julie here to discuss the reunion plans. Were they here yesterday?"

Mary Lou filled another napkin dispenser. "I don't think so. At least not during the day. But let me ask Myra. She worked the night shift."

Mary Lou used her cell phone to punch the woman's number. "Myra, did you see Suzy Turner or Julie Kane in the diner yesterday?" A pause. "No? All right. Thanks."

She hung up and turned to Amanda. "She said they didn't come in last night."

Amanda frowned. If the emails had been a lure, the assailant could have caught them outside. But how would the unsub force two women to go with him? Or her...

And where had the perp taken the women?

As soon as Justin returned to the counter, the waitress sat the food he'd ordered on the counter. Amanda appeared next to him, grabbed the glass of water and sipped it.

"Suzy and Julie weren't here yesterday."

Justin gestured for her to sit down and eat. "I checked out back just in case but didn't see anything."

Her features softened in relief, and she sank onto

the stool and picked up her burger. "I've been thinking about the possibility of a female suspect. We need to talk to the school counselor and the cheerleading coach."

"Eat and then we will." Justin dug into his food ravenously.

Amanda dipped a few fries in ketchup and inhaled them, then retrieved her phone and punched in a number. Seconds later, she spoke, "Lynn, this is Sheriff Blair. I need to talk to you ASAP. It's urgent. Please call me back."

"No answer at her place either?"

Amanda shook her head. He hoped that wasn't a bad sign.

They finished their food in silence; then he reached for the bill. Amanda reached for it at the same time, and their fingers touched. A current of awareness shot through him, and his gaze was drawn to her mouth. She flicked her tongue out to lick away a drop of ketchup, and hunger bolted through him.

The memory of that kiss teased at his senses.

Hell, he could become obsessed with her mouth.

If they weren't working together, looking for a murderer, he might give in and take her to bed. Get his fill so he could put her out of his mind.

Once would do it. No, twice. Maybe three times.

Dammit. She was getting to him bad.

"I've got it," he said, his voice harsher than he'd intended.

She jerked her hand away. "Fine. I'll meet you at

the car." She headed toward the ladies' room, and he forced himself not to watch her hips sway as she walked.

He paid the bill and left a nice tip, then strode outside. Sunset had long come and gone, and the town was quiet.

As if nothing bad had ever happened in Sunset Mesa.

Not as if a murderer had been kidnapping and killing young women for a decade.

"I called and talked to Deidre Anderson, the cheerleading coach," Amanda said when she got in the car. "She's expecting us."

Amanda drove two streets over and turned into a small neighborhood with stucco houses. A bicycle and skateboard had been left in the drive, indicating the woman had teenagers herself.

They walked to the door in silence, feeling tension that had as much to do with the heat building between them as it did the case. Maybe it was more intense because of the case and the fact that Justin was afraid Amanda might be targeted next.

Justin knocked, and a slender woman who was wearing a warm-up suit and had ash-blond hair opened the door. "Hi, Amanda," she said. "You must be the Texas Ranger who was at the school today. I'm Deidre Anderson."

"Sergeant Justin Thorpe. Thanks for letting us stop by. Can we come in?"

"Please." She gestured for them to enter and five

minutes later they were seated at a modest kitchen table with coffee.

"How can I help?" Deidre asked.

"It's about Kelly's death." Amanda filled Deidre in on the information they had on the missing-persons case so far and their speculations about Donald Reisling and his father.

"We've been operating under the assumption that the killer is male," Justin said. "But I saw an unidentified female disguised as a cleaning woman enter Suzy Turner's apartment last night, so we are considering the possibility that we might be looking for a female."

Deidre stirred sweetener into her coffee, then added a hefty amount of hazelnut creamer. "I don't understand how I can help."

"We found some evidence linking the girls' disappearances to the class reunion at the high school, so we've been looking at the students from that graduating class, their connections and any enemies who might want to target them. That's the reason we wanted to talk to you."

"A photo of the cheerleading squad was used as Suzy's screen saver," Amanda explained. "It started me thinking that perhaps a classmate at the time, a girl who tried out for cheerleading and didn't make it, might have harbored a grudge against the ones on the squad."

Justin sipped his coffee. "Can you think of anyone who fits that description?"

"Gosh." Deidre traced a finger along the rim of her mug. "There are girls who try out and don't make it every year. It's hard for me to remember ten years ago." She walked over to a bookcase, pulled a yearbook from the shelf and flipped through it. "I can't imagine anyone being so angry over not making the squad to kill because of it."

"It was most likely someone who already had emotional problems. Maybe someone from a bad home life," Amanda said. "She probably suffered from low self-esteem."

Deidre sank into a chair and continued thumbing through the yearbook. She paused at a photograph of the cheerleaders at a pep rally, then seemed to be scrutinizing the teens gathered on the stands.

Her finger paused on a brunette in the second row who wore thick glasses and had buck teeth.

"Hmm, I do remember this girl trying out. Her name was Bernadette Willis. I think I cut her the first day. Poor girl just wasn't coordinated."

Or pretty enough, Justin thought. "How did she handle the rejection?"

"She seemed upset, but so did the other girls who didn't make it."

"Why does she stick out to you?" Justin asked.

Deidre tapped the photo again. "It's just…I faintly remember something about her family, that her father had run out on her and her mother that year."

"What about the mother?"

"She was an alcoholic. Crashed her car into a tree

a few weeks after the father left. Bernie had to live in a group home for teens after that."

Amanda heaved a breath. "Her whole life fell apart," Amanda said. "Then she was dumped into the system. No telling what happened to her there."

AMANDA STRUGGLED TO recall if she and Bernie had shared any classes together. Maybe chemistry or biology lab? She faintly remembered rumors about her having emotional problems, that she was angry all the time.

They needed to talk to the school counselor, then maybe the social worker, and find out all they could about her.

If she'd suffered some kind of breakdown, it might explain why she'd started exacting her revenge.

Amanda's phone buzzed, sending a wave of fear through her. She checked the number, her chest clenching as she answered. "Sheriff Blair."

"Sheriff, it's Eileen Faust. You have to get over to the event center."

"What's wrong, Mrs. Faust?"

"Suzy Turner…I found her here and… Amanda, she's dead."

## Chapter Seventeen

"We have to go, Justin," Amanda said. "That was Lynn Faust's mother. She found Suzy Turner's body at the event center."

Deidre gasped. Justin's jaw tightened as he stood.

"Let us know if you think of anything else, Deidre," Amanda called over her shoulder as she and Justin rushed to the door.

A gusty breeze hit her as she stepped outside, and a hint of rain scented the air. She couldn't believe that Suzy was dead, too.

How many more women had to die before she stopped this maniac?

Her hand trembled as she tossed Justin the keys. "You drive. I'm going to try and reach Julie and Lynn again on the way."

Justin jumped in, started the engine and called for a crime team and the ME as he backed out of the Anderson driveway.

For once Amanda was glad to have someone else to rely on. She felt frail and vulnerable and…as if she'd failed.

Emotions welled inside her, threatening to overflow.

But she had to maintain control. When she found this unsub and had him—or her—in custody, then she could fall apart.

Justin maneuvered through the subdivision and turned onto the road leading into town. She punched Julie's number again, but, just as she'd feared, no one answered, so she left another voice mail.

Next she tried Lynn, and got her voice mail, as well. "It's Sheriff Blair. It's important I talk to you, Lynn. You may be in danger. Call me immediately."

The event center slid into view, and she pointed it out to Justin. "Park in the lot on the left."

Justin veered into the space, turned to her and placed his hand on hers. "If you need me to handle this, I can, Amanda. I understand that you knew these women and their families and that this case is tearing you apart."

Tears burned the backs of Amanda's eyelids, but she blinked them back. The last time she'd cried had been at her father's funeral. She couldn't break down now.

"I did know them. That's why I have to stop this madness." The temptation to hang on to his hand fluttered through her, but she had to resist.

Suzy's mother was waiting for news. News that was not going to be what she wanted to hear because Amanda had failed to find this psycho.

If Julie and Lynn died, their blood would be on her hands, too.

JUSTIN CURSED AS he climbed from the squad car. Amanda was blaming herself, but Suzy's death was just as much his fault as hers.

He should have figured out who this perp was by now. Instead, he felt as if they were chasing leads all over town. First Terry Sumter, then Donald Reisling and his father, then Carlton Butts's brother and now this Bernadette Willis was a suspect.

The fact that Amanda hadn't been able to get hold of Julie or Lynn meant they might already be in trouble.

Dead on his watch.

Amanda straightened her spine as they approached the front door of the building, but a middle-aged woman wearing a white skirt and sweater rushed out, her face streaked with horror and tears.

"Sheriff, it's so awful," she cried. "Suzy…she's in there…. Why would someone do this?"

Amanda paused to calm her, her voice soft. "I'm so sorry, Mrs. Faust. When did you find her?"

"Right before I called you," she said, hysteria lacing her voice. "What's happening in this town? First Kelly Lambert and now Suzy! And that horrid mess at the school. Who's doing this?"

"We're doing everything we can to figure that out," Amanda said firmly.

Justin tried to telegraph to her that it would be all right.

But both of them knew that was a lie.

The town's residents, more specifically the young

women of Sunset Mesa in Amanda's very own grad-uating class, were being targeted by a killer who was growing bolder by the minute.

"How did the killer get into your building?" he asked.

Mrs. Faust pressed two fingers to her forehead as if thinking about the question. "I don't know. I didn't have anything here today, so I stopped by tonight to drop off some flower arrangements for a luncheon we're having tomorrow."

"What type of luncheon?" Amanda asked.

"It was a mother-daughter event, one we set up every year to honor the mothers and daughters the day before the reunion begins. The country club mothers put it together."

"So not every female in the class is invited?" Amanda said. "Just the ones whose parents belong to the club?"

Mrs. Faust wiped at her eyes. "That's right. Why? Does that mean something?"

"It means whoever left Suzy's body here chose this spot to make a point just as they chose the school," Justin said.

"Because he or she felt left out of the group," Amanda pointed out.

"Stay here with her," Justin told Amanda. "I'll go in and examine the scene. Send the crime scene team and ME in when they arrive."

Justin headed inside to check out the body. He heard Amanda asking about Lynn as he entered the building, then only the echo of his footsteps as he walked across the slick marble floor. The exterior of the building was nondescript, but the inside was upscale. White tablecloths were draped over several round tables and more rectangular serving tables jutted up against the wall. Silver and china plates had been set, rose-colored napkins tied with white lace atop the plates and bouquets of fresh roses filled a cart, obviously centerpieces waiting to be distributed.

The room looked formal and classic, just waiting for the socialites to adorn it.

Except for the dead body perched in a sitting position on a dark green velvet sofa on the stage.

Justin had never seen Suzy Turner in person, but in her photograph she was a pretty girl. Yet the green eyes that had been lit up in the photograph were now wide, glazed with shock and fear, and her normally olive skin was pale with death.

He yanked gloves from his pocket and inched toward her, a wave of anger and sadness hitting him. Suzy Turner might have made mistakes as a teenager; maybe she'd even been mean to some guy or girl. But she had been a kid ten years ago and didn't deserve to die and be left like this.

He knelt and brushed his hand across her cheek in a silent apology, giving her a moment of quiet reverence before he did anything else.

Swallowing back emotions, he examined her neck. The same type of bruise pattern indicated she'd been strangled with a man's belt. Her dress looked disheveled, probably from the killer moving her body, but again there was no visible evidence of sexual assault.

Heart hammering, he checked her hands. One lay across her heart as if the killer had positioned it there, while the other dangled open by her side.

Using his cell phone, he snapped some photos of her exact body position and the area, then lifted her hand from her chest and slowly uncurled her fingers.

Just as he'd expected, inside lay a class ring.

He lifted it up and examined the inside and saw the initials JK.

Julie Kane.

Was the killer sending a message that Julie Kane was next?

AMANDA FELT MRS. FAUST'S horror deep in her bones. "Listen to me, Mrs. Faust. I promise Sergeant Thorpe and I will find out who did this. But right now, I need you to talk to me. Did you see anything out of the ordinary when you arrived? An open window? Broken lock? A car leaving the place?"

"No, no," Mrs. Faust murmured. "The parking lot was empty. I don't know how the killer got in. Maybe he broke the lock."

"Did you touch anything when you went inside?"

"The door," she said. "The kitchen counter in the back room." She looked frazzled. "Maybe the walls. I brought the flowers in the back door, then put them on the cart to move them to the ballroom. That's when…I found Suzy." She gripped Amanda's arms. "Does Suzy's mother know?"

Dread balled in her stomach. That would be the worst part. "Not yet. I'm going to send my deputy out to tell her while Sergeant Thorpe and I investigate."

"Do you know who did it?" she cried.

"We have a couple of suspects we're interviewing. I need to ask you something else." ·

Fear deepened the grooves around her mouth. "What?"

"Have you seen or talked to Lynn today?"

Mrs. Faust shook her head. "No, we spoke yesterday. She was shopping for a dress for the dance Saturday night, then she said she was going to meet Suzy…" Realization dawned, and the woman gasped. "My God, no…"

Her legs buckled, and Amanda caught her before she collapsed. She eased her down on the front steps to the building and urged her to take deep breaths.

But the woman's fingernails dug into Amanda's arms. "You think this maniac has my daughter?"

"I don't know, but I called and left her a message to phone me ASAP. Where does she live?"

"In Austin," Mrs. Faust said. "But she's been staying at the inn in town. A couple of her friends were supposed to be coming in tonight, and they wanted to be together. It was Julie Kane's idea." Her voice cracked. "Lynn said it would be like old times, a big slumber party."

Amanda's throat thickened. "Keep trying to call her and let me know if you hear back. Maybe she and her friends are out shopping and having dinner and took in a show or something."

She prayed that was true, but her gut instinct warned her it wasn't the case. She remembered her conversation with Deidre Anderson. "Mrs. Faust, do you remember a classmate of ours named Bernadette Willis?"

The woman's eyebrows bunched together. "Just that the mother was a drunk. Someone in town said the daughter was crazy, too. That she had to go to some kind of juvenile delinquent home before she came here because she tried to kill her mother."

Amanda's heart stuttered. If that was true, it meant Bernadette had a history of violence.

She might be the unsub they were looking for.

JUSTIN GREETED THE crime scene team and ME, the sight of Suzy's body giving the team pause as it had him.

"How did the killer get her in here without anyone seeing or hearing something? This building is right on the edge of town," Lieutenant Gibbons said.

Justin had already checked out the exits and entry points. "I took a look around. There's a back exit that connects to the parking lot. He probably waited until it was dark. There are no surveillance cameras, and apparently no security system."

Unbelievable for a place that catered nice events, but it was a small town and everyone knew everyone else, so Mrs. Faust had probably thought they were safe.

"Look carefully—even a hair might be able to help us nail this perp," Justin said. "And keep in mind that we may be looking for a female."

"What makes you suggest that?" Dr. Sagebrush asked.

Justin explained about Bernadette Willis and the cleaning woman at Suzy's condo complex.

The crime scene team went to work snapping pictures and searching the room. Another tech went outside to rope off the area as a crime scene. They wouldn't be having the luncheon here tomorrow.

Amanda entered, her mouth in a grim line.

Emotions darkened her face at the sight of Suzy, a battle raging for control in her eyes.

"She was strangled?" Amanda asked.

"MO is the same as Kelly and Tina," Justin said. "The ring in her hand belonged to Julie Kane."

Amanda muttered something beneath her breath. "Lynn and Julie were staying at the Sunset Mesa Inn. Mrs. Faust hasn't heard from Lynn since yesterday. She was supposed to be shopping for a dress for Saturday night."

"Did you talk to the inn's manager?"

Amanda clenched her phone. "Next on my list. Then I want to talk to the school counselor."

One of the crime techs motioned that he'd found something, and Justin walked over to him and saw him holding up a long brown hair with a pair of tweezers. "The victim is blond. You may be right. This may belong to the unsub, a female."

Or hell, this was an event center; there was no telling how many people had been in and out. They probably needed the names of all the employees, vendors, cleaning staff. Another list to sort through.

"Bag it and anything else you find. And don't forget to search the door and floor for prints. If our suspect is female, she probably had to drag the body inside. At some point, she might have touched the wall or floor for support."

Amanda returned, her phone in hand. "Neither Lynn nor Julie showed up at the inn last night. I told the owner to call me if they did. And I asked my deputy to check out the rooms where Lynn and Julie were staying to see if there was any indication where they might be."

"I'll call and put a trace on Julie's and Lynn's phones." He punched in the number for his chief and made the request as he and Amanda rushed to her car. This time she took the wheel and, ten minutes later, they were seated in the living room of Faye Romily, the school counselor.

"I don't understand how I can help you," Ms. Romily said.

Amanda explained the connections they'd made between the missing girls and the recent murder victims.

"You really think one of your classmates is behind this because of some deep-seated jealousy?" Faye asked.

"The unsub has to be mentally unstable," Justin explained. "The class reunion was a trigger for the rage that has been eating at him or her for years, so the perp escalated."

"Deidre Anderson said that Bernadette Willis was cut from the cheerleading squad that year, and that she suffered emotional issues."

A stricken look crossed Faye's face, and she stood and wrapped her arms around her waist. "Amanda, you know I can't discuss the sessions I had with any of the students. That's confidential."

Amanda sighed wearily, but Justin squared his shoulders. "Ms. Romily, we believe there are two other young women missing now. If the suspect follows the pattern, those girls may be dead before morning. We don't have time for a court order—"

"Please, Faye," Amanda said. "You don't have to divulge details—just tell us about Bernadette. Did she suffer emotional problems?"

Faye inhaled sharply and gave a quick nod.

"Did you think she was dangerous?"

"I don't want to say—"

Justin cut in, "Did she ever talk about hurting anyone in her class?"

Faye winced and cut her eyes sideways. "She was a troubled young girl. I…tried to follow up and see what happened to her after graduation and was told she was institutionalized at one point."

"Do you remember the name of the hospital or mental-health center?"

Faye hesitated a moment, then scribbled it down on a piece of paper.

Amanda flashed Justin a look of concern. They both were watching the clock.

"I'll call them," Justin said. "See what they'll tell me or if they have an address where she lives now."

Amanda's phone was buzzing. "That's the mayor calling. I'm going to tell him to set up a press conference for the morning. I think it's time we inform everyone what's going on and warn them there's a serial murderer in town."

Justin punched the number for the mental hospital. How many more women did the unsub plan to kill?

## Chapter Eighteen

Justin punched Disconnect on the phone with a curse. "The receptionist at the hospital wouldn't tell me anything about Bernadette. Patient confidentiality."

"Let's go there in person," Amanda said. "Maybe if we talk to one of the doctors they'll help us. I'll start working on a warrant."

Justin gritted his teeth as she put in the request and drove toward the mental hospital.

"Yes, Judge, we think two more women may be missing and possibly dead. Every second counts." A pause, then Amanda thanked him and hung up.

"He's going to do it. I set the press conference up for ten in the morning."

"Hopefully we'll have the killer in custody by then and you can deliver some good news."

She rolled her shoulders as if to relieve tension. "From your lips to God's ears."

She accelerated, and ten minutes later they parked at a concrete building set off from the road surrounded by barbed wire fencing.

"This place looks like a prison," Justin muttered.

"It's the only mental health facility within a hundred miles," she said. "I guess they have some dangerous cases."

"Like Bernadette?"

She shrugged, and they identified themselves at the security gate, then parked in the visitor lot. Other than the few cars in the employee lot, the place looked virtually empty.

Justin glanced at the clock. Of course, it was late for visitors. But he had the uneasy sense that this was a place where unwanted people were discarded by loved ones and forgotten.

His impression of the place continued to go downhill as they entered. The building smelled old, like sick people, medicine and despair. Amanda squared her shoulders as she spoke to the receptionist, who eyed Justin over the rims of her bifocals.

"Judge Stone is working on a warrant for your records on Bernadette Willis. I need to speak to the director of the hospital and the doctor who treated Bernadette."

The nurse fiddled with a pencil stuck in her bird's-nest hair, then punched a button and paged the director along with a Dr. Herbert.

The director arrived first, a portly man with a white beard, and led them to his office. Seconds later, Dr. Herbert, a rail-thin fiftyish bald man appeared, reading glasses perched on his head.

Justin explained the reason for their visit.

"We need to know everything you can tell us about Bernadette," Amanda said. "What was her diagnosis?"

"You know I'm not comfortable discussing my patients," Dr. Herbert said staunchly.

"We are investigating the disappearance of a string of girls, at least three of whom are dead," Justin said in a dark voice. "If Bernadette exhibited signs of violence or verbally threatened any of them and you don't tell us, then you'll be responsible for their murders."

Dr. Herbert and the director exchanged concerned looks; then the director gestured for Herbert to speak up.

Dr. Herbert fiddled with the pocket of his lab coat. "Bernadette was suffering from bipolar disorder when I treated her. Our sessions were private and yes, she did express hatred for several of her teen-age classmates, girls she felt shunned her and made fun of her, but as far as I know, she didn't act upon that aggression." He paused, and Justin and Amanda both remained silent, waiting for more.

"What aren't you telling us?" Justin finally asked.

Dr. Herbert released a wary sigh. "She did attack another girl who was here at the time."

"What do you mean, she attacked her?" Amanda asked. "What exactly happened?"

Dr. Herbert tensed. "She tried to strangle her."

AMANDA'S ADRENALINE KICKED in, charging her with hope. "What happened after that?"

"We reevaluated her and changed her medications," Dr. Herbert answered. "She received intensive therapy and was released a year later."

"Where did she go from here?" Justin asked.

Herbert slanted the director a questioning look. "I referred her to a home for troubled young women so she could continue her recovery with group therapy."

"What was the name of the place?" Amanda asked.

"Hopewell House."

Justin cleared his throat. "Did you follow up with her?"

Dr. Herbert shrugged. "I did. But I was told she left after a couple of weeks. I have no idea where she went from there."

Amanda ground her teeth. Bernadette could have moved anywhere.

"You should try her aunt," the director said. "She visited her once in the hospital, but said she was too old and that Bernadette had too many problems for her to take her in permanently."

Amanda's heart constricted. So Bernie had felt abandoned and alone. Even her only living family member hadn't wanted her.

"Do you have her contact information?" Amanda asked.

The director drummed his fingers on the desk. "I'm not supposed to give it out."

"Do you want more women to die?" Justin asked bluntly.

The man scraped a hand over his beard, then jotted down the address.

Amanda shook their hands. "Thank you for your help. If you think of anything else that might be of use, please call me."

She jangled the keys in her hands as they rushed to the car. Seconds later, she peeled from the parking lot and headed out of town toward the aunt's house.

"What do you remember about Bernadette?" Justin asked.

"Not much. She was quiet, withdrawn. Obsessed with science fiction characters and movies. Rumors circulated that she was really a guy."

"Was she gay?"

"I don't know. Her clothing and mannerisms and hair seemed masculine."

"Gender confused," Justin suggested. "Maybe she was struggling with her sexual identity and the popular girls accentuated the fact that she didn't fit in."

Amanda swerved onto a side road that seemed to lead nowhere. Raw land and rugged countryside sprawled ahead of them, an eerie feeling encompassing her.

Bernie's aunt lived out here—alone?

The car bounced over ruts in the road, a sliver of moon offering little light against the shadows. Her headlights blazed a trail on the dirt road that finally led her to a small trailer. No other houses or trailers were around, making her wonder why the woman lived in such an isolated area.

"What's the aunt's name?" Justin asked as she parked and they walked up to the door. The trailer was rundown. A clothesline out back held a string of ratty jeans and housedresses, and a mangy-looking dog lay slumped on the ground near the stoop.

"Oda Mae Willis. She is Bernie's father's sister. I heard she is eccentric, that she never married."

Three cats also roamed the yard, and when Amanda knocked, a screeching sound like cats fighting echoed from the inside. Shuffling followed. Then the door squeaked open, and a stoop-shouldered gray-haired woman wearing an orange flowered housedress stood on the other side. The scent of cigarette smoke surrounded Amanda, and the acrid smell of cat urine wafted through the door.

Amanda fought back a gag. "Ms. Willis, it's Sheriff Blair and this is Texas Ranger Sergeant Thorpe."

The woman glared up at her with rheumy eyes. "What you want?"

"We need to ask you about your niece. Is she here?"

"Hell, no," the woman muttered. "I told those folks at the hospital I couldn't take her in. That girl's too much trouble."

Amanda's heart squeezed for Bernadette. First to lose her parents, then to be a misfit in school, and to have her aunt refuse to give her a home. "Have you seen or talked to Bernadette lately?"

The woman clacked her false teeth. "Hadn't seen her in years and she just showed up here a couple of days ago. Said she was back for that reunion. Wanted to show all those kids that was mean to her what she'd made of herself."

"What was it she wanted to show off?" Justin asked.

"Hell if I know," Oda Mae muttered. "But she had that mean look in her eyes like she did the night I sent her to that hospital."

"You sent her there?" Amanda asked.

Oda Mae's head bobbed up and down. "Didn't have no choice. She killed one of my cats. Strangled the poor baby to death. Then she started on another and I got my shotgun and made her stop."

Amanda's pulse clamored. Killing animals was a sign of sociopathic behavior.

An indication that Bernie might have been practicing for killing a human.

And becoming a serial killer.

"If Bernadette isn't staying with her aunt, where would she stay?" Justin asked as they settled back in the car.

Amanda rubbed her finger along her temple and started the engine. "The inn is the most popular place." She punched the number for the inn, then asked if Bernadette was registered there. "Okay, thanks. If she shows up, please call me." When she hung up, she shook her head.

"There are a couple of motels on the outskirts of town. Try those."

She gave Justin the names and he made the calls. The first one was a bust, but the clerk who answered at the Canyon Resort Motel confirmed that Bernadette was registered in room twelve.

Amanda steered the car back onto the dirt road, then hung a left when she reached the main highway. Five miles down the road, they reached an adobe building painted a burnt orange that boasted a view of the canyon. Amanda parked, and they rushed to the lobby.

They both flashed their credentials. "We're looking for Bernadette Willis," Justin said.

The tiny lady behind the counter looked as if she were ninety. "What's going on, Sheriff?"

"We just need to talk to her. Do you know if she's here?"

"Saw her leave this morning."

"Can you give us a key to her room?" Amanda asked.

"I don't think I'm supposed to do that," the little woman said.

"Look, we need to get in there. We have reason to believe she might be in danger," Justin said, hedging.

Fear splintered the lady's face, and she reached behind her and retrieved a key. Her hand trembled as she handed it to Amanda.

Justin led the way outside and down the row of rooms until they reached room twelve. He knocked and identified them as police officers, but no one answered so he used the key and let them inside.

The room was dark, and he flipped on a light by the door.

"Bernie?" Amanda called as she brushed past him to check the bathroom. But there was no answer. The bed was unmade, a duffel bag tossed on the floor, a wet towel thrown across the bed.

Justin scanned the rest of the room and saw a yearbook on the bed. He picked it up, his pulse clamoring as he flipped the pages. He found the photo of the cheerleading squad on Suzy's screen saver.

Bernadette had drawn big black x's across the girls' faces.

Amanda's phone buzzed, and she snatched it from her belt. "Sheriff Blair." She hesitated. "Okay, we'll be right there."

"What?" Justin asked.

"That was Delores at the inn. Bernadette is there now."

Justin flipped the yearbook around. "Look at this."

Amanda took one look and motioned to the door. "Let's go. If we hurry, maybe we can arrest her tonight and this ordeal will be over."

AMANDA SWUNG THE squad car toward town, hit the gas and wove around a tractor trailer pulling out from a side street.

Her thoughts strayed to Lynn and Julie. Were they all right?

She hoped they'd snuck away to the city for a while.

The other option was too disturbing because it meant they might be dead.

But if she had them, why go to the inn tonight?

The temptation to turn on the siren hit her, but she didn't want to warn Bernadette she was coming.

Justin pointed to an SUV across the street from the inn. "Look, there's a black SUV with a brunette in it."

Amanda slowed and parked several cars back on the side of the road. "Come on, let's move in quietly."

Justin slid from the car, his gun drawn, and they crept along the sidewalk toward the SUV. They inched past a sedan and a minivan. Then Justin gestured that he'd take the right side of the SUV and she'd move in on the left.

A car whizzed by, forcing her to duck between cars, and Bernie glanced up in the mirror. Panic flashed in her eyes when her gaze met Amanda's in the rearview mirror.

She reached for the keys, and the car engine rumbled to life. Amanda didn't intend to let her get away. Keeping low, she ran toward the SUV. Justin reached it before she did and tapped on the passenger side of the vehicle.

His knock distracted Bernie long enough for

Amanda to reach the driver's side. She rapped on the driver's door, but Bernie saw her and gunned the engine.

Amanda had to jump back to keep from getting run over. "Stop, Bernie!"

Justin gestured toward the squad car, and they jogged back to it. Amanda jumped in and floored the engine. Tires squealed as she chased the SUV through town and onto the country road leading toward the motel.

Another car darted onto the highway in front of Bernie, and she swerved to miss it. She lost control, and the car wove back and forth, brakes squealing.

Amanda slowed to avoid hitting her as the SUV careened into a ditch.

Amanda's breath caught. If Bernie died, they might never find the other missing women.

## Chapter Nineteen

Amanda steered the car to the side of the road and cut the engine, and she and Justin ran toward the SUV.

By the time she reached it, smoke was billowing from the hood. Justin beat her to the driver's side, yanked open the door and dragged Bernie from the vehicle.

Blood dotted her forehead and lip, and her eyes looked glazed. From drugs or shock?

Amanda gripped her phone. "I'll call an ambulance."

Justin eased Bernadette down onto the ground a few feet away from the SUV and checked her pulse.

Amanda punched 911 and gave the dispatch officer an address, then knelt beside Justin and Bernie. "How is she?"

"Her pulse is low and thready, and she's banged up, but the air bag worked, so she might be all right."

Amanda noted a few differences in the girl she'd once known. Gone was her pointed nose; instead she had a petite rosebud of a nose. Her teeth had been straightened, her coke-bottle glasses were gone and…she had implants.

Was this what her aunt had meant about Bernie wanting to come back and show off what she'd made of herself? That she was a beauty now, not the geeky masculine awkward teen they'd made fun of.

"Bernie." Amanda caught Bernie's hand in hers. "Can you hear me?"

Bernie gave a low groan; then her eyelids fluttered. Wild panic darted through her eyes.

"You've had an accident," Amanda said. "The ambulance is on its way."

Bernie reached her hand up to touch her face as if to make sure her remodeling hadn't been affected.

"You're fine," Justin said. "Just some bruises from the air bag. But the medics need to check you out."

"Why did you run?" Amanda asked.

Bernie's lips quivered, making Amanda's stomach knot.

"You were outside the inn," she continued. "Were you looking for Julie and Lynn?"

Bernie coughed, wincing as she gripped her chest in pain. "They wouldn't let me stay there," she growled. "Stupid jerks haven't changed at all."

"Is that why you made all those girls disappear over the years?" Justin asked. "Why you killed Kelly Lambert and Suzy Turner?"

Bernie hissed through clenched teeth. "They deserved to die. All of them…they deserved exactly what they got."

THE AMBULANCE ROARED to a stop and two medics jumped out. Amanda directed them to Bernadette.

"This woman is a suspect in a homicide so I need to ride with her," Justin said.

The blond medic checked Justin's badge while the dark-haired one hurried to Bernie and took her vitals. He instructed Amanda not to let her move; then he and the second medic retrieved the stretcher, secured Bernie's neck with a brace and boarded her.

"I'll ride along if you want to meet us at the hospital," Justin said.

Amanda agreed, her expression torn. "I'll search her car and find her phone and meet you there."

Justin climbed in beside Bernie, hoping to solicit a confession on the way to the hospital.

But the minute the doors slammed shut, she closed her eyes and clammed up.

"Bernadette," he said in a gentle voice. "If you abducted Julie Kane or Lynn Faust and they're still alive, you need to tell me now. Things will go a lot easier on you if we find them alive."

She opened her eyes and gave him a cold stare.

"The D.A. can cut you a deal for their safe return. And we can arrange psychiatric care instead of putting you in a maximum-security prison."

A blink of her eyes was her only response.

"Think about it," Justin said as the ambulance careened around a curve and into the hospital emergency room entrance. "A psychiatric hospital versus a prison with murderers, rapists and gangs."

A sinister smile curved her lips. "They deserved to die," she said again. "Every single one of them."

Justin urged her to say more as the ambulance screeched to a stop, and the medics pulled the stretcher from the ambulance. But she maintained her silence.

Was she the sociopath who'd committed all these crimes?

By the time Amanda arrived, they'd carried Bernadette off for X-rays and a CAT scan. The two of them went to get coffee and Amanda paced the waiting room while they waited on Bernadette to be moved to a room.

"Did you find a gun in her car?" Justin asked.

"No." Amanda lifted her cell phone. "I've been checking her calls but so far, nothing we can use against her. And no calls to any of our victims."

The doctor entered and cleared his throat. "She's going to be all right. She sustained a blow from the air bag, but no broken ribs. We'll watch her overnight for a concussion." His brows arched in question. "We did a tox screen, and it showed that she is taking medication that's used to treat bi-polar disorder."

"She was a mental patient at one time," Justin filled in.

"That explains it," the doctor said. "Do you know who her doctor is?"

Amanda relayed their conversation at the mental hospital. "We're putting her under arrest," Amanda

said. "I'm sure the court will order a psych evaluation. I'm assigning my deputy to stay at her door all
night. But I want to talk to her again before I leave."

Justin followed her inside, and they found Bernadette sleeping.

"Damn, Bernie," Amanda said, her tone laced
with irritation. "Have you been kidnapping and mur-
dering our classmates all these years?"

But Bernadette had lapsed into a deep sleep and
didn't respond.

"I offered her a deal," Justin said. "But she just
reiterated that the girls deserved to die."

"No, they didn't," Amanda said fiercely. "There
are a lot of jerks in high school, but people grow up
and some of them change."

Justin rubbed his hands down her arms in a soothing gesture. "You have to remember that she's mentally ill, Amanda. Her thought processes don't work
like a normal person's."

Amanda knotted her hands into fists. "She has
to wake up and tell us where Julie and Lynn are."

A knock sounded at the door, and the deputy
poked his head in. "Reporting for duty, Sheriff."

Amanda updated him on the situation. "Make
sure she stays handcuffed to the bed. I want to question her if she wakes up."

He claimed a seat in the vinyl chair in the corner.
"I'll call you the minute she stirs."

"Thanks."

Justin checked his watch as they left the hospital.

It was midnight already. They'd been working non-stop since he'd arrived in town. Something nagged at the back of his head as she drove from the hospital though.

Julie and Lynn were still missing. And he'd wondered if Amanda was a target.

Was she safe now that Bernadette was in custody?

AMANDA PARKED AT the station, her adrenaline waning, and Justin retrieved his SUV.

Clouds rolled above, obliterating the moon as he followed her to her place. Amanda kept reliving the past few days, seeing the dead girls' bodies in her head.

Bernadette had been cunning enough to remain under the radar for years. But now that she was in custody, they could hope the town would be safe again.

But they still needed to find Julie and Lynn and the bodies of the other missing victims.

Weary, she parked and walked up her porch steps, aware Justin was close behind her. She could feel his big body, his strong presence, his intensity…

She halted on the porch, her heart stuttering. A picture had been tacked on her door.

One of her cut out from her class yearbook. A big X had been drawn across her face.

A deep shudder coursed through her body.

"What the hell?" Justin snarled.

"It's a message to me, that I was going be next," Amanda whispered hoarsely.

Justin yanked gloves from his pocket, tugged them on and removed the photo from the door. "If she left her prints on it, this will help us build the case."

"Bag it and we'll send it to the lab tomorrow," Amanda said. "We need to check in with them and see what they found at the event center, too."

Even though they had Bernadette in custody, she removed her weapon before unlocking the door. Behind her, Justin did the same and she slowly crept inside.

Everything looked just as she'd left it, yet she had the uneasy sense that someone had been inside. She visually swept the attached kitchen while Justin eased his way to the hall and her bedroom.

"Clear," he called.

She walked to the bedroom and looked inside, then checked her bathroom. "It doesn't look like anything's been touched."

"She's taunting you, wants you to know she's watching."

"She wanted to kill me, too," Amanda said, the truth harsh. "For some reason, she lumped me with that group even though I wasn't a cheerleader or dancer or part of their crowd."

"Maybe she thought you were protecting them."

"That could be," Amanda admitted.

Justin pulled her near him, his dark gaze raking over her. "Bernadette is a sick woman. No one could have predicted what she would do." He tucked a strand of hair behind her ear, and her heart fluttered with a feminine awareness that she rarely felt.

It was probably just the situation, she told herself. She was upset. Women her age had died all around her and she'd been helpless to save them.

"Amanda," Justin said in a husky whisper. "You're nothing like the students who were mean to Bernadette. You know that, don't you?"

Her chest ached with suppressed emotions. "But I should have seen how disturbed she was." Her voice cracked. "The people in town depended on me to solve this case instead of letting it go on so long."

Justin stroked her arms with his hands, making her want to lean into him.

"You did solve it. Bernadette is handcuffed, and we'll get her confession in the morning and find out where Lynn and Julie are." He lifted her chin with his thumb. "Not only did you do a good job, but you showed compassion to the victims and their families. That's a lot more than some law enforcement officers do."

Her breath caught as she looked into his eyes. For a brief second she felt totally vulnerable, feminine, wanted.

Desire heated the air between them, desire charged by emotion, danger and adrenaline from the case and horrors they'd seen.

Desire that made her forget all her reservations.

Pulse throbbing, she laid her hand against his cheek. Coarse beard stubble grazed his jaw and his lips were thick, parted as if hovering, waiting for a kiss.

She answered him by rising on her tiptoes and pressing her lips to his.

RAW HUNGER BLAZED through Justin as Amanda fused her lips with his. She was tough but tender, smart but vulnerable, shy yet aggressive. A mixture of sensuality that fueled his desire with an intensity he'd never felt before.

Some part of his brain shouted at him to stop this madness, but the week had been filled with another kind of madness that made him crave this kind. A physical connection charged with want, need and passion.

He deepened the kiss, teasing her lips apart with his tongue. She moaned and captured his face between her hands, moving against him in a seductive torture.

Wind whistled behind them, and he realized they'd left the door open. He kicked it closed with his foot, then trailed his hand down Amanda's side. When his hand hit her holster, he paused.

"Amanda?"

She murmured a soft whisper of need against his lips, then dropped her hands and unstrapped her holster. He quickly did the same, and they set their weapons on the end table.

The plush rug in front of her fireplace beckoned, and he threaded his hands into her hair and kissed her again, leading her to the rug, where they knelt, slowly undressing each other in a seductive tease.

Even in a uniform, she was beautiful, but in red satin panties and a sheer lace bra, she was exquisite. Her hair fell around her bare shoulders, inviting him to play in the tangled strands, and the rise of her chest as she exhaled with desire drew his eyes to the soft flesh above the lacy cups of her bra.

He dipped his mouth and tasted her skin. Succulent. Sweet. Heady.

She moaned and stripped his shirt, buttons popping in the breathy silence, the heat between them igniting as he lowered his mouth to tease her nipples through the lace. Her breasts were larger than he'd expected, her nipples dark, achingly enticing. He cupped them in his hands, molding them and lifting them so he could tease the turgid peaks before he stripped the bra and held her bare in his hands.

"You're so beautiful, Amanda," he rasped.

"You feel so good," she whispered as she unsnapped his jeans and pushed them down his hips.

His length surged and hardened, aching to be free, inside her.

Desperate for her touch, he helped her shuck his jeans and then she was climbing on top of him, pushing him back against the rug, straddling him and stroking him.

His sex throbbed, begging for release, but he

moved her hand and shifted her hips so he could strip her panties. Her hair fell around her face like a curtain as she bent over him and kissed his neck.

Erotic sensations flooded him, but a moment of rationality returned, and he reached for his jeans, grabbed a condom from his pocket and ripped it open. Amanda helped him roll it on, her eyes darkening as she straddled him again and lowered herself onto him.

He gripped her hips, barely hanging on to control as his length filled her. With a whispered sigh of pleasure, she rotated her body, moving up and down on top of him in a frantic rhythm. The friction was erotic, her body a haven for him as he thrust deeper and deeper.

She braced her hands on his chest, her breath gushing out with a moan as her body quivered. Euphoria carried her away, and she moved faster and faster, circling her hips and riding him until his own orgasm teetered on the surface.

He tugged one nipple into his mouth, suckling her until she cried out his name, and they rode the wave of pleasure together.

AMANDA GROANED, HER body convulsing, every nerve cell in her alive with erotic sensations. Justin gripped her hips, pumping deeper inside her until colors exploded behind her eyes and she soared over the edge.

Her breath rasped out, and she clutched his shoulders, savoring the feel of his thickness inside her.

She had never felt more complete. More...of everything. Pleasure blended with emotions, making her throat close as feelings for Justin overpowered her.

Fear immediately seized her.

She could not have feelings for him. He was a Texas Ranger married to his job just as she was. He could die on the job just like her father had.

And then she'd be left behind again, alone and... broken.

Instincts warned her to stop this foolishness now. To forget that she'd needed him and that he'd seemed to want her just as much as she wanted him.

That it was the best sex she'd ever experienced.

But that was it—just sex. Yes, just sex.

Sex was normal. A tension release. They were two consenting adults simply working off the strain of the past few days.

As long as she kept their lovemaking in perspective.

She should pull away.

But when she looked down into his passion-glazed eyes, and hunger heated his expression, she couldn't make herself leave the rug.

Justin must have felt the same way and wanted her to know the sex meant nothing because he rolled her sideways, then stood up and strode into the bathroom.

She closed her eyes, reminding herself that they

were on the same page, but disappointment made unwanted tears swell in her eyes.

She wanted him again.

The door creaked open, and she took a deep breath, expecting him to leave. Instead, he crawled back onto the rug with her, slid his arms around her and spooned her.

Amanda wanted to turn around and kiss him again, but forced herself to lie still.

Just for tonight, she'd let him hold her.

It was already Friday. One more day until the reunion.

One more day until the town would see that they couldn't stand by and let innocent teenagers be bullied and brutalized and tormented.

They thought words couldn't hurt a child. But words could be cruel and cut a frail person to the bone just like a knife could.

Anticipation rose, exhilarating and sweet. Ten years of watching those who'd sinned climb their way to the top in spite of their shortcomings.

This week they'd returned to brag and gloat as if the ones they'd trampled on didn't matter.

But they did matter.

Tomorrow when they gathered to celebrate, they would be talking about funerals and goodbyes and the end of their glory days.

And justice would finally be served.

Julie and Lynn would attend that party, but they wouldn't be dancing.

No...dead girls didn't dance.

## Chapter Twenty

Justin started to leave Amanda's bed a half dozen times during the night. But each time he'd felt her lush, warm body against his and hadn't been able to bring himself to go.

Because he wanted her again.

They had made love over and over during the night. Finally they'd slept.

Both of them had been exhausted from the investigation and the tension had triggered their need for raw sex.

Nothing more.

*Then why don't you want to walk away?*

He climbed from bed, unable to answer that question because the answer terrified him. Because he was starting to care for Amanda.

She turned over and murmured his name, and he lowered his head and kissed her. "Time for reality. That press conference is this morning. And I need to question Bernadette again."

Her so-called confession had haunted him during

the night. She'd said the girls deserved to die. But she'd never actually admitted that she'd killed them.

He needed to grill her for details. Make sure they had the right unsub.

Amanda's life depended on it.

THE MENTION OF the press conference drove thoughts of another lovemaking session with Justin to the back of Amanda's mind. She heard her shower kick on, and she was tempted to join Justin, but with daylight streaming through the window, she had to face reality and the truth.

She and Justin were coworkers who'd relieved their stress in bed together. It happened.

She'd get over it.

Hoping to end the nightmare today, she dragged on a T-shirt, then went to the kitchen to make coffee. Her stomach growled, and she checked the fridge, then pulled out eggs and bread and whipped up some French toast.

Finally the shower turned off, a relief as it was much too tempting to think of Justin naked in there alone. When he entered the kitchen, his hair was damp, and he looked sexy as hell.

God help her. She was seriously falling for him.

His dark gaze met hers, stirring erotic memories of the night before. His jaw tightened as he glanced at the table, and she suddenly wanted to forget breakfast and make love on the table.

He cleared his throat, hunger flaring in his eyes as

if he'd read her thoughts. But the look faded and his professional mask fell back over his chiseled face.

"Thanks," he said. "I'm starving."

So was she. But not for food.

Still, she kept that comment to herself. Couldn't invite more personal interaction today. They had to finish this case.

So she handed him a mug of coffee and set their plates on the table. Still, the ordinary routine felt intimate, his masculine body taking up all the air in the room.

He wolfed his food down, then studied her while he sipped his coffee. "I'm going to question Bernadette, make sure we tie up details while you hold the press conference."

His statement made her refocus. "I've been thinking about that," she said. "Maybe I should postpone and go with you. We need to find out what she did with Lynn and Julie."

He shook his head. "No, go ahead with the meeting. The town has to be up in arms now and panicking. Talking to them is the right move. But I wouldn't reveal Bernadette's name."

"I don't plan to," she said. "But I do want to urge people to come forward if they have any information." She stood, carried her dishes to the sink and rinsed them.

"I'll clean up while you shower," Justin offered.

Unaccustomed to having a man in her kitchen, she rushed to the bedroom to get ready for the day.

After the conference, a family picnic was scheduled to jumpstart the reunion.

She wanted to be there and study the group just in case they were wrong about Bernadette.

Hopefully Lynn and Julie would show up safe and sound.

As soon as she finished showering and dressing, she phoned her deputy to check on Bernadette.

"She slept like the dead all night."

"Sergeant Thorpe will be there soon to talk to her. When he arrives, go home and get some rest. I'm heading to the office to hold a press conference with the mayor."

An hour later, she stood with the mayor in front of the county courthouse and greeted the media. Reporters immediately hurled questions at her.

"What's happening in Sunset Mesa?"

"Did you find the missing girls?"

"Is this a serial killer?"

Amanda held up her hand in the universal signal for them to hold the questions. "At this point, we do believe that the disappearance of several women from this town and neighboring counties is related. The bodies of three victims have recently been found—Tina Grimes, Kelly Lambert and Suzy Turner. Police believe that they were kidnapped and murdered by the same perpetrator and that the upcoming ten-year class reunion at Canyon High triggered the perpetrator to escalate."

Hands shot up, but she waved them off and continued. "We do have a suspect in custody although I'm not at liberty to disclose the name yet as we're still investigating. That said, there are still other women missing at this time. If you have any information regarding the whereabouts of Lynn Faust and Julie Kane, please call my office immediately."

"How were the women murdered?" someone shouted.

"Do you think Lynn Faust and Julie Kane are dead?"

Amanda gritted her teeth. "As I said, if anyone has any information, please call my office immediately."

She glanced at the mayor and turned to duck inside so he could smooth ruffled feathers, but another shout echoed behind her.

"What if you have the wrong person? What if the women in town are still in danger?"

Amanda slowly turned around to see who'd voiced the question and frowned at the sight of Kelly Lambert's maid of honor, Betty Jacobs. "Are we still in danger, Sheriff?"

Amanda wanted to tell the young woman no, that she was sure they had the right perpetrator. But she couldn't lie. And if she assured the residents and her former classmates they were safe and another woman was abducted, it would be her fault.

"All I can say is that we have a suspect in custody. Until we confirm that this person is the one we've been looking for, I would urge all the women in town to be on guard. Travel in pairs and don't trust anyone."

JUSTIN BROUGHT A mini recorder in with him to see Bernadette. The deputy sheriff met him at the hospital room door.

"I talked to Sheriff Blair and told her the suspect has been asleep all night."

"She didn't wake and say anything? Talk in her sleep?"

The deputy shook his head. "They must have given her some heavy-duty drugs. Not a peep all night."

"Thanks. I'll handle it now."

The deputy left, and Justin stepped inside and closed the door. He walked over to the bed and studied Bernadette. Granted, she had suffered emotional problems and had killed her aunt's cat, but was she a serial murderer?

Considering her emotional issues, did she have the organizational skills and patience to wait months before abductions and to commit this many crimes without being caught?

He touched her hand. "Bernadette, it's time to wake up and talk."

Her eyes suddenly popped open as if she'd been faking sleep. They looked cloudy, hazed with drugs, but the same sinister smile he'd seen the night before stretched across her face.

"Talk to me," he said in a low voice. "You came

back to town for the reunion to show off your new face, didn't you?"

"Yes," she murmured. "But do you think those bitches cared?"

"But *you* cared, didn't you? You've been angry since high school. You decided to start taking your revenge out on them ten years ago."

Bernadette reached for the water on the steel table beside the bed, and he handed it to her. She took a long sip, then laid her head back down.

"They should have noticed," she said. "Should have let me stay at that inn. But they thought they owned the school, and now they think they own the town."

"That's wrong," he said. "I understand why you're upset. They hurt you ten years ago and now they're still doing it."

"I wasn't the only one," Bernadette said. "There were others. The geeks like me. Like Carlton Butts. You know he killed himself because of them."

"Yes, I heard that. But you decided to fix yourself and to make them pay instead of committing suicide."

"They're not worth dying for."

"But they deserved to die. You said that."

"Yes, they deserved to die."

"So you practiced killing with your aunt's cats?"

Bernadette's eyes widened. "You talked to that mean old hag?"

"You hated your aunt, didn't you? Like everyone else, she abandoned you."

"She loved those damn cats more than she did me. She threw me out, but she kept taking in those mangy strays. They pissed all over the place. Her trailer smelled like garbage and cat urine, but she chose that over me."

"She hurt you so badly that you killed one of her cats. Then the teens at school wronged you, so you retaliated by abducting and killing them one at a time."

Bernadette twisted sideways, clutching the sheet to her neck.

"You can talk to me here or down at the station," Justin said. "Either way, Bernadette, you have to tell me what happened. I'm on your side."

She pierced him with a look of rage. "You're not on my side. No one is."

"I can stand up for you if you tell me what happened. Who was the first girl you abducted?"

She looked down at her fingers where they were wrapped around the sheet. "I took them all, made them suffer for what they did."

Suffer? She'd strangled them, but there was no evidence of torture or sexual assault. Or that the victims had been beaten.

"How did you make them suffer?" he asked.

She chuckled. "You know how. You found Kelly and Suzy."

"You humiliated them by leaving them in public

places. But Tina's body was found in a creek. What about Melanie and Avery and Carly and Denise? Why didn't you leave their bodies for us to find?"

"Because I had more on my list who had to pay." A bitter laugh sounded. "And it was fun watching the police run in circles."

He narrowed his eyes. "Who was the first one you took?"

She shifted restlessly, then rubbed her temple as if she had to strain to think. "I don't know, I get them all confused. It's been a long time."

"Avery Portland, wasn't it? Or was it Melanie Hoit?"

A heartbeat passed and Bernadette breathed deeply. "Avery was supposed to be at the school dance."

"But she disappeared and no one heard from her again," Justin said. "And Melanie?"

"From the mall. She was a shopaholic. A rich daddy's girl." Her eyes hardened. "Everyone wanted to be like Melanie."

"What did you do with their bodies?"

Bernadette looked him straight in the face then gave a small shrug. "I don't remember."

"How did you kill them?"

Her eyes darted sideways. "I told you I made them suffer."

"How? Did you beat them? Stab them? Torture them before you ended it?"

"I choked them," she said. "I watched them beg

for another breath, but I took it away." She snapped her fingers. "And just like that, they were gone. The world's a better place without them."

"What about Gina Mazer? Where did you abduct her?"

Bernadette pinched the bridge of her nose. "I told you I can't remember them all. They were all alike, one blending into another." Her eye began to twitch. "The stupid meds the doctor gave me…they make me forget."

Or maybe she wasn't the killer. Because there was no one named Gina Mazer in the case files.

"So now you're ready to finish it," he said quietly. "You're ready to go public. You did all this for the glory, to prove something. You can't do that, Bernadette, if you don't let everyone know you're responsible."

"Then tell them to take my picture and put it all over the news. Bernadette Willis finally gets payback for the abuse she suffered."

Justin hesitated. "Okay, but for the record, you have to tell me how you carried out the crimes."

"I told you I choked them."

"How?" Justin pressed. "With your hands? A scarf? A rope?"

Bernadette began picking at her fingernails. "With a scarf. One I took from my aunt's house. It smelled like cat urine. I wrapped it around their throats and squeezed it so hard they choked on the odor."

A hysterical laugh echoed from her, and Justin silently cursed.

Either Bernadette was just plain crazy and wanted to taunt him with her sadistic games.

Or...she hadn't killed the women.

Because the killer had used a man's belt to strangle the victims. That was one detail they'd held back from the press.

The one detail that only the police and the real killer knew.

THE POLICE HAD a suspect in custody. Some classmate of all the dead girls named Bernadette.

Another one of the odd ducks in school. One those mean girls had picked on.

Bernadette understood the reason they'd had to die.

Maybe when this was over they could be friends.

## Chapter Twenty-One

Justin met Amanda at the reunion picnic, surprised she'd shown up wearing her uniform.

"You trying to make a statement to your former classmates?"

She shrugged. "Yes, that they're safe. And that I'm on the job."

"Not here to mingle."

"Not here to mingle," she said in a wry tone. They walked across the field by the lake. Dusk was setting, the ducks nibbling for food at the edge of the water, a breeze stirring the trees and whipping Amanda's hair around her face.

He wanted to reach up and tuck it behind her ear, but they were in public and he couldn't touch her. Although he imagined making love to her again tonight and need speared him.

*Not a good idea, man. One night was just sex. Two could lead to something more, could mean she is getting in your head.*

*And your heart.*

No one got into his heart.

"What happened with Bernie?"

Justin chewed the inside of his cheek. "I don't know, Amanda. She wants credit for the crimes, but when I asked her about the details, there were discrepancies in her story."

Amanda paused by a tree and looked up at him, her eyebrows furrowed. "What do you mean?"

"She claimed the drugs made her memory foggy. I threw in the name of a fake victim to test her. And she said she couldn't remember all the names."

Amanda shaded her eyes with her hand as she scanned the picnic area and pavilion where her former classmates and their spouses and kids had gathered. Grills were heating up for burgers and hot dogs, and one of those bouncy houses had been set up for the kids, along with face painting, music and games.

"It is possible that the medication messed with her memory," Amanda said. "Of course that will make it harder to get a conviction unless we find other evidence to support her story."

And so far, they hadn't. "When I asked her how she killed the girls, she said she choked them to death with a scarf."

Alarm flared in her eyes. "Not a belt?"

"No."

She pursed her lips. "Maybe she's trying to throw us off with the details because she still has plans for Saturday night."

"That's possible. Either way, we have enough to hold her for twenty-four hours."

"She wouldn't tell you where Julie and Lynn are?"

He shook his head. "They haven't turned up at the picnic?"

"No. But I'll keep watch." She headed down the hill. "I guess I should canvass the crowd in case anyone's heard from them."

Justin had a bad feeling that the women were dead.

The question was—where were their bodies? And if Bernadette hadn't murdered them, who had?

AMANDA THREADED HER way through the throng of classmates, listening to the normal chitchat about how much everyone had changed, or hadn't, the questions about marriage and kids and jobs. She remained on the periphery, avoiding engaging in conversation, listening and hoping for information that might help with the case.

Because if Bernadette wasn't the murderer, one of her other classmates might be.

Or was Bernadette just toying with them now? Dragging out the inevitable to make them wonder and throw suspicion off of herself?

Two of Kelly Lambert's bridesmaids cornered her by the sodas. "We saw the press conference," Anise said. "You found the person who killed Kelly?"

"Who was it?" Mona Pratt asked.

"I'm sorry, but I can't divulge that information yet," Amanda said.

Anise touched her arm, her voice pleading. "But you're sure you have him in jail?"

"We think so," Amanda said, then because these women might be in danger, added, "but until we have the evidence we need to confirm that we have the right person in custody, please be careful. This killer targeted our classmates. Watch your backs."

Worry darkened both women's faces. "Is that why Julie and Lynn aren't here?" Mona asked. "You think they're dead, too?" Panic strained her high-pitched voice and several other people turned to her with questioning eyes.

Amanda lowered her voice. "I don't know, but if you hear from them, please call me."

She moved to the edge of the crowd, feeling as out of place as she had ten years ago.

But that feeling reminded her that the killer felt the same way. So she sipped her soda and watched the picnic—old friends reconnecting and rehashing memories, the couples introducing spouses and children, and the occasional whisper and somber expressions of sorrow and regret that several of the students at Canyon High had died or disappeared and were presumed dead.

But as she studied the faces, she didn't see anyone who looked suspicious. Carlton's brother was there, laughing with a couple of guys he used to run track with. Donald Reisling sat in his wheelchair, although he wasn't alone. Three of the former basketball players were crowded around him asking for financial advice, listening raptly to what Donald had to say.

Raymond Fisher, the man who had been Kelly's fiancé, had even shown up although he and Terry Sumter passed each other with mutinous glares.

Then Renee cornered Raymond, hovering close, obviously consoling him for his loss.

WHEN JUSTIN AND Amanda left the picnic, they wanted to move Bernadette to the jail. But the doctor who'd treated her had called for a psych evaluation, and instead they transferred her to the psychiatric ward to stabilize her medication.

While Justin called the crime lab to check on forensics and to ask if the tech team had found any leads on Julie's and Lynn's phones, Amanda called her deputy to ask him to stand guard by Bernie's room again that night.

Amanda didn't know whether it was the meds or if Bernie had realized that she wasn't going free and that, if she'd planned another murder for the big reunion Saturday night, that she wouldn't get to follow through, but apparently she'd shut down again.

When she and Justin arrived back at the sheriff's office, Lynn Faust's mother was waiting along with Julie Kane's parents.

"Where are our daughters?" Lynn's mother cried.

"You said you arrested someone. Where is he?" Mr. Kane demanded.

Mrs. Kane swiped at tears. "Let us talk to him. Maybe he'll tell us where our daughters are."

Lynn's mother clutched her arm. "Please, Amanda, please find them. Lynn's all I've got."

Emotions thickened Amanda's throat. "We're doing everything we can."

"Damn you, Sheriff, it's not enough." Mr. Kane raised a fist and shook it in the air. "Tell us who kidnapped our daughters, and I'll get him to talk."

Justin rapped his knuckles on the desk. "Listen here, everyone. We understand you're upset, but the sheriff is doing her job. We do have a suspect and are continuing to question her—"

"It's a woman?" Mrs. Faust shrieked.

"Let us see her!" Mr. Kane shouted.

"I can't do that," Justin said, kicking himself for mentioning the suspect's gender. "But I promise you as soon as we know anything, we'll inform you."

"But our babies are still out there…" Mrs. Faust sobbed.

Mrs. Kane leaned into her husband. "We have to know what happened to them. Julie, she was so bright and smart… She can't be gone."

Their grief ripped at Amanda's heart, and she silently vowed that somehow she would find the answers the families sought.

Even if it meant finding Julie's and Lynn's bodies so they could bury them and put them to rest.

BY THE TIME Justin managed to coax the families to leave, he knew Amanda was wrung out. He saw the guilt and pain in her eyes, and felt helpless to do anything about it.

Because he wasn't sure they had the right unsub.

Meaning Amanda might be in danger and wouldn't be safe until the perp was caught.

He suspected tomorrow as the big day, the reveal—if the killer had one. That Julie's and Lynn's bodies would turn up in some way connected to the reunion so all their classmates could bear witness.

And so Amanda would feel even worse.

The CSI team had found little. Nothing to connect Bernie to the crimes. Her cell phone showed calls to the inn and motel, but not to Julie, Lynn, Kelly or Suzy. If she'd used a burner phone, it hadn't been in her purse or car.

Together he and Amanda made rounds in the town, checked the inn again to see if there had been any word from the women, then picked up some dinner from the diner and drove back to Amanda's.

Tension vibrated between them, the uncertainty hovering around Bernie and the case needling both of them. Once they ate, Amanda poured herself a drink and offered him one.

He liked a woman who drank brown whiskey.

He liked Amanda period. She was strong and gutsy and fought for her town.

Worn and worried though, she looked vulnerable

again. He sipped his whiskey with her on the porch, the night sounds echoing around them.

The memories of the night before taunted him.

He wanted her again.

Amanda sighed and leaned against the rail, looking out over the woods and canyon, and he couldn't help himself. He stepped up behind her, needing to hold her, aching to pull her into his arms and touch her everywhere.

To make her sigh and moan with pleasure and erase the dark shadows in her eyes.

He gently stroked the hair from her cheek and pressed a kiss behind her ear. Amanda leaned back into him and whispered his name softly, a protest to stop. A plea for more.

He took her hand and led her inside, then swept her in his arms and carried her to the bedroom, where they stripped and made love all through the night.

FOR A FEW blissful short hours, Amanda felt at peace. Safe. Cared for. As if everything might be all right.

But daylight brought reality and uncertainty. When the case ended, Justin would leave Sunset Mesa. His job carried him all over Texas. She understood that from her father.

She also understood that he might not come back.

Daylight also reminded her that Julie and Lynn were still missing. And that Bernadette might not be the killer.

Justin joined her in the kitchen for coffee and breakfast again, the two of them silently agreeing not to discuss the frantic sex they'd had during the night.

"Let's question Bernie again," she said as they cleaned up the kitchen.

Justin nodded, and they drove to the hospital, the tension between them vibrating with dread. The reunion dance was tonight.

The tick tock of the clock was like a time bomb echoing in her ears.

If Bernadette wasn't the suspect, then they could expect trouble tonight. The killer probably had something big planned for today. Plans that didn't involve celebrating the good times from years past, but adding to the death count and celebrating her revenge.

Amanda led the way to the psych floor and they identified themselves to the head nurse, who escorted them to Bernie's room. Bernie was sleeping, her face pale beneath the hospital lights.

Amanda shook her gently. "Bernie, I need you to wake up and talk to us."

Bernie made a low sound in her throat, then slowly opened her eyes. Gone was the wild, panicked, angry look. Her eyes looked flat, empty, as if she was far away.

"Bernie, it's Sheriff Blair. Amanda," she said, hoping to connect with her on a more informal basis. "We need to talk."

Bernie pushed hair from her face and looked around, disoriented. "Where am I?"

"The hospital in Sunset Mesa," Amanda said. "Yesterday you told us that you killed Suzy Turner and Kelly Lambert. That you've been punishing classmates who were mean to you."

Her eyes darted back and forth. "I didn't say that. You're lying."

"You told me they all deserved to die," Justin said. "That you choked them."

"No," Bernie bellowed. "I didn't. You're making up stuff to have me locked up again."

"That's not true," Amanda said. "You were at the inn. You—"

"I didn't do anything wrong!" Bernadette yelled. "I didn't kill anyone."

The hospital door suddenly opened, and a barrel-chested doctor rushed in. "What's going on?"

"They're saying I killed someone!" Bernie shouted. "They want to lock me up. It's just like before, everyone turned against me."

The doctor gestured for Amanda and Justin to step outside, and a nurse rushed in and gave Bernadette a sedative to calm her.

"I'm afraid she needs intensive therapy," the doctor said.

"But yesterday she ranted about killing several women," Justin said.

"Bernadette has taken heavy medication for years. She suffers from delusions. When she's off her meds as she was yesterday and probably has been for days, she doesn't know what she's saying."

"She was in a delusional state when we brought her in?" Amanda asked.

He nodded grimly. "Off her meds, she's susceptible to suggestions from others. If you'd told her she was a green alien, she probably would have agreed."

Amanda knotted her hands into fists. "So we can't believe anything she said yesterday? And even if we did, it would never hold up in court."

A sliver of unease rippled through her. She and Justin had both doubted whether or not Bernie's confession had been real.

Now she had even more doubts.

Which meant that the killer might still be out there planning to snatch another victim.

She watched the group decorating the float, laughing and talking and reminiscing about the fun times they'd had.

High school was supposed to be the time of your life.

But for some it had been torture.

They added strings of crepe paper and made a papier-mâché school mascot, even fashioned the canyon for which the school had been named out of clay and paper.

One of the women laughed as she placed two dolls in cheerleading uniforms on the float while a young man planted a football in the middle of the football field onstage.

Tonight that float would sit outside the dance for everyone from Canyon High to see. It was tempting to leave Julie and Lynn in place of those stupid dolls.

But she had another plan. The big finale.

Then Amanda Blair had to die.

## Chapter Twenty-Two

Tension knotted Justin's muscles as he waited on Amanda to dress for the dance. He had changed into clean jeans and a blue Western shirt, but he strapped on his gun and covered it with his jacket.

When Amanda stepped from the bedroom, she looked so stunning she robbed his breath. In deference to the occasion, she wore a short black dress that hugged her curves and made her look more like a sex siren than the sheriff.

She rubbed her hands down her hips in a self-conscious gesture. "Too much? I'll go change." She turned to go back into the bedroom.

He caught her arm. "No, you look beautiful."

"I don't care about that," she said. "I have a job to do."

He chuckled. "Perhaps you'll look less intimidating dressed up for the reunion. Your uniform might spook the killer if she's there."

"The killer will be there," Amanda said with conviction.

He silently agreed and walked her out to his SUV. "I'll drive tonight."

"Maybe my car should be there. It might make the other guests feel more secure."

"You'll be there," Justin said. "And so will I. We'll stay on our toes."

Except at the moment, all he wanted to do was strip that slip of a dress and make love to her again.

God, he was like a sinking ship. He not only liked and admired Amanda—and she was the best sex he'd ever had—but he wanted to protect her tonight. Lock her here where she'd be safe, off the killer's radar.

But he couldn't even suggest that. Amanda wouldn't go for it, and it would be unprofessional of him.

He squeezed her hand as they settled in the SUV. "Amanda, you know the killer left that photo of you on your door as a warning."

She lifted her chin. "I know. The unsub wants to punish me, too."

"That means you're in danger," he said in a hoarse voice. "I don't want you to get hurt."

She lifted the hem of her dress and he saw the gun strapped to her thigh. It was the sexiest thing he'd ever seen.

"I'm a pro," she said. "Don't worry about me."

But he did worry about her, and that scared him. Caring might make him sloppy and distracted.

He couldn't afford that. Not tonight.

THE CRIME SCENE techs had released the event center in time for the dance, but the committee had decided to move the party to another venue, a hotel ten miles north with a ballroom. Lynn's mother had recommended the place, saying she couldn't have a party at the center where Suzy's body had been found, especially not when her own daughter was missing.

Volunteers from the school committee had scurried to decorate the place and make the arrangements. The float classmates had created was parked in front, a testament to the class that they were honoring the past and refused to allow the recent traumatic events to stop them from celebrating their friendships.

When she and Justin entered, a band was playing, the lights were low and couples filled the dance floor.

She had opted not to attend the dinner before the party, although she and Justin had staked out the outside, watching to see if anything went wrong.

She scanned the room, looking for anything suspicious.

"You look different out of uniform."

Amanda turned to see Donald looking up at her from his chair.

"I'm still on the job though." She sipped her club soda. "What about you, Donald? Are you enjoying seeing the old crowd?"

He shrugged. "I'll never forget how some of them treated me after the accident. But it's nice to be vindicated in that I made a success out of myself in spite of them."

"Good for you," Amanda said, wondering if she'd been wrong about Donald.

Across the room, she noticed Carlton's brother dancing with Eleanor Goggins, one of Kelly's bridesmaids.

Near him, Raymond Fisher stood talking to Renee Daly, his former girlfriend and one of their original suspects. The couple looked chummy, raising Amanda's doubts again. Was Renee simply consoling him, or did she have another agenda?

Suddenly a commotion broke out near the door, and a small crowd gathered. Justin squeezed her arm. "Stay here and keep an eye on everyone. I'll check it out."

Amanda's nerves prickled, and she wove through the room, studying the faces of the people she'd known as teenagers, hating that she was now viewing them as possible murderers.

Her phone dinged that she had a text and she slid it from her purse and checked it, expecting to see a message from Justin.

But the text was from an unknown.

She squinted in the dim lighting, her heart hammering as she read the text.

I have information on the killer you're looking for. If you want to know who it is, meet me in the stairwell.

Amanda jammed the phone back in her purse, then scoured the room for Justin to tell him about the message, but she didn't see him anywhere. He must still be outside.

Determined to follow up, she wove through the dancers and people hovered around the bar and ducked through the back exit to the hallway. She veered down the hallway toward the dark stairwell.

When she reached it, she heard a muffled footstep, then the brush of clothing, as a shadow appeared from the corner. Something shiny glinted in the darkness. A gun.

Shock immobilized her when she recognized the person aiming the weapon at her.

JUSTIN SHOULDERED HIS way through the shouting and voices outside the ballroom exit, then jogged over to where a small crowd had gathered.

"What's going on?" he asked one of the young men.

The guy pointed to the right. "Someone trashed the float."

Justin inched his way closer and saw two women about to climb on the float. "Who would do such a horrible thing?" someone cried.

"We have to get those dolls off the float," the other one shouted.

"Wait." Justin caught up with them and gently grabbed the first woman's arm. Then he saw what had upset them. Two dolls in cheerleading clothes were set up on a football field on the float. But their clothes looked as if they were covered in blood and the dolls had been hung by their necks from the goalposts.

"This may be related to the crimes in town. We'll need to examine it." He addressed the group. "I don't want anyone to touch this float." He gestured toward one of the men. "Get one of the security guards. I need him to watch this until the crime team arrives."

The gentleman jogged toward the door to the ballroom while Justin tried to quiet the crowd. He circled the float searching for anything else out of place. A knife. Forensic clues. A note or photo of some kind.

But he saw nothing else out of the ordinary. The hair on the back of his neck prickled, and he scanned the group outside in search of someone on the periphery watching.

The killer was here. She wanted to enjoy her classmates' reactions.

But the group had thinned, milling back into the dance. The guard approached, and he explained that he needed him to cover the float while he phoned for a crime team. Of course dozens of hands, maybe a hundred, had touched that float so it would be hard to weed out the killer's prints. But maybe she'd messed up and they could find some forensic clues on the dolls.

He punched in Lieutenant Gibbons's number while he hurried inside to tell Amanda and monitor the group. But he didn't see Amanda anywhere. He explained to the lieutenant that he needed a crime scene unit, then tried Amanda's number, but she didn't answer.

Anxiety mounted.

The only reason she wouldn't answer was if there was trouble.

He spotted Betty Jacobs, one of Kelly's friends, and approached her. "Have you seen Amanda?"

She shook her head no, and he moved along the bar asking others.

"She was heading toward the stairwell a few minutes ago," Donald said. "She received a text and rushed out of the room."

Justin thanked Donald, then rushed into the hallway toward the stairwell. The area was dark, but he noticed something shiny on the floor below the stairs. He bent down, a seed of panic sprouting.

Amanda's gun lay on the floor by the wall. Scuff marks marred the floor leading toward the back door.

The killer had been here. And he or she had Amanda.

AMANDA SILENTLY CURSED herself for letting the woman get the jump on her with the gun. Of all the people she'd suspected, it had never occurred to her that Carlton Butts's mother had been vindictive or strong enough to carry out a series of crimes for ten years.

But the woman had coldly shoved a pistol to Amanda's head, then tied her hands behind her back and was shoving her into an old van. "I thought you had trouble walking."

"And I thought you were Carlton's friend, but you were just like the others. You deserted him when he needed you."

"I didn't mean to do that," Amanda said. "I cared about him."

"Then why have you been running all over town trying to stop me." The woman's eyes blazed with rage as she slammed the door shut, jumped in the front of the van and sped from the parking lot.

"Because killing those women isn't right," Amanda said, hurling herself to a sitting position in the backseat as she struggled with the ropes behind her back.

"You know how they treated my son," she snarled as she took the curve on two wheels. "They killed him."

"I understand how you feel and that you're angry," Amanda said. "But Mrs. Butts, a lot of teens and kids get picked on. Not all of them commit suicide."

"No, some of them go in and shoot the bitches," she said. "But my Carlton was too sweet for that. But they drove him crazy, drove him to such despair that he never thought anyone would like him, much less love him."

She sped down the highway, mumbling incoherently about each one of the women she'd hurt and what they'd said and done to her son. "He was a bright boy, so smart," she continued on a rant. "He could have been something one day. You know he loved science. He might have worked on one of those space stations or discovered a cure for some rare disease."

Amanda worked at the knot behind her back, slowly threading the end through the loop. "I think he could have done that, too," she said. "But he gave up, Mrs. Butts. He made the choice not to fight back and—"

"Don't you dare badmouth my son," Mrs. Butts cried. "See, you're just like the others. All you care about is your life, like he never existed at all."

"That's not true," Amanda said. "I mourned for Carlton and still do. I've never forgotten what happened to him. That's one reason I chose law enforcement. So I could help others."

"But you took up for those mean girls who hurt Carlton. I saw you on the news. You made out like they were innocent, like they never did anything wrong."

"We found Tina, Kelly and Suzy," Amanda said, knowing her time might be running out to find the information she needed. "What did you do with the other bodies? With Melanie, Denise, Avery, Carly... how many have you killed?"

"Just the ones who deserved it," Mrs. Butts said, her voice brittle. "And don't you worry. All of the early ones are together. All in one big grave."

A shudder of horror ripped through Amanda. Mrs. Butts sounded demented. "Except for Tina. I thought someone saw me with her so I left her in that river. That was a mistake. But I had to get rid of her fast." Mrs. Butts cackled. "I thought she'd just float away. Bye-bye, bye-bye."

"But she didn't and the fish ate at her body," Amanda said. "That was cruel."

A nasty laugh escaped the woman. "Cruel? Do you know what she did to poor Carlton? She sent him a note that she wanted to meet him behind the bleachers in middle school. He thought she wanted to kiss him, but she pulled his pants down, then tied him to the bleachers and left him for the whole class to see."

Amanda's heart hurt at the story, her hand aching from tearing at the rope. So far, it hadn't budged. "What about Julie and Lynn?"

Mrs. Butts threw the van to the right and raced down the drive to the canyon behind the high school.

A cold chill enveloped Amanda. She knew exactly where the woman was going and why.

She was going to kill her at Carlton's Canyon, where her son had taken his life.

## Chapter Twenty-Three

Justin retrieved Amanda's weapon and stuffed it in the back of his jeans as he ran to the back door and glanced outside. Except for a couple of vendor vans, the back lot was empty.

He scanned the hallway and stairs but didn't hear or see anything. Frantic, he raced back into the ballroom. The first person he saw was Donald Reisling. Could Reisling's father have come after Amanda?

Shoulders tense, he grabbed the microphone from the DJ and tapped it to get everyone's attention. "Listen up, folks. The prank outside with the decimated cheerleader dolls was a diversion. Someone abducted Amanda—I mean Sheriff Blair. She supposedly received a text and went into the hall. Her gun was left on the floor so someone either overpowered her or had a gun. Did anyone see her?"

"The last I saw she was going into the hallway," Donald said.

"I saw her near the stairs," a young woman spoke up.

"Was she with anyone?" Justin asked.

He glimpsed Carlton's brother sneaking out the side door and yelled at him to stop. "Where do you think you're going?" Justin vaulted off the steps and lunged at him. "Did you do something to Amanda?"

Ted shook his head, pain lining his face. "I've been in here with Debby all night."

"He has been with me," a buxom redhead said. "I swear."

Anise ran over, her breath rasping. "I didn't see Amanda, but I saw Carlton's mother near the stairs."

Justin narrowed his eyes at Ted. "Your mother is here?"

"I...didn't know she was," Ted said in a choked voice.

Justin grabbed the young man by the collar. "But you know something. Now spill it."

Ted shook his head in denial, but emotions shrouded his features. "It can't be. My mother... she's messed up, but she wouldn't hurt anyone..."

"She wasn't using her walker either," Anise said. "She was actually standing upright."

A muscle jumped in Justin's jaw. "Your mother faked her handicap?"

Ted scraped his hand over his goatee. "I...don't know, I'm sorry. I didn't think...didn't want to believe that she'd hurt anyone."

"She never recovered from Carlton's suicide," Debby said in a whisper.

"Where would she take her?" Justin asked.

Ted rubbed his goatee again. "I...have no idea."

"Let's try your house. You can call her on the way."

He shoved the young man outside to his SUV and roared from the parking lot.

He hoped he'd find something at Wynona Butts's house to tell them where the woman had taken Amanda.

He had to hurry before Mrs. Butts killed her.

He couldn't lose her now.

AMANDA'S LUNGS CLENCHED for air as she spotted Julie and Lynn beside the drop-off for the canyon.

They were alive.

"Mrs. Butts—Wynona—you can stop this now," Amanda said as the crazed woman yanked her from the car and shoved her toward the other women.

"You're going to watch them die," she hissed, "then you'll join them."

Amanda fought with the rope. She had one end through the loop. Now if she could just loosen it and slip her hands free.

Wynona nudged her forward with the gun at her back.

"Is this where you dumped the other bodies?" Amanda asked.

A cynical laugh echoed behind her. "It was fitting, don't you think? They've been lying at the bottom, looking up at the school where they tormented my son."

Nausea rose in Amanda's throat. All this time,

all these years, the missing women had been dead, their bodies lying in the elements.

So close to home yet no one had known. And the families had no answers.

Julie and Lynn both looked up at her with terrified eyes. Their hands and feet were bound, their mouths gagged and Carlton's mother had secured them to a tree with thick ropes.

Amanda tried to communicate to the women that she'd save them. She didn't know how, but she'd die trying.

Surely Justin had realized she was missing. Somehow he'd find her. She had to stall.

Wynona pushed her to her knees beside Lynn and Julie. Tears streamed down Julie's cheeks. Lynn made muffled sounds of fear and protests behind her gag.

"Tell me how you did it," Amanda said to Wynona. "How you managed to trap your victims over the years."

Wynona cackled again. "It was easy. I met them in different places, mentioned Carlton." She gestured at herself. "With that walker, none of them suspected a thing. Stupid twits."

"They thought you were an innocent grieving woman," Amanda said, disgusted at the depth of the woman's depravity.

"And you...Carlton looked up to you, Amanda. He thought you'd be his friend forever." She placed the barrel of the gun at Amanda's temple. "But you let him down worse than everyone else. I think that's what sent him over the edge. Now you have to die."

JUSTIN DROVE LIKE a madman to Wynona Butts's house while Ted frantically phoned his mother. But she didn't answer, and when they arrived at the house, there was no car in the drive.

He hit the ground running.

"Why didn't you tell someone what your mother was doing?" Justin snapped as Ted let him in the house.

"I told you I didn't know," Ted said, panicked. "You aren't going to hurt her, are you?"

Justin glared at him. "I'm going to do whatever necessary to stop her from killing Amanda."

Justin shouted to identify himself as he and Ted entered the house.

"Look around, see if your mother left any indication where she might take Amanda."

Justin jogged into the woman's bedroom, searched the desk in the corner, then the dressers, but found nothing but old bills and clothes.

Desperate, he swung open the closet door, his chest heaving at the sight inside. Mrs. Butts had cut out pictures of all the victims from the yearbook and taped them on the back of the door with big black X's marked across the faces just like the one she'd left on Amanda's door.

Then he noticed a photograph of Carlton when he was a teen. Beside it was another picture, this one of the canyon behind the school, more specifically a grassy area by a tree where she'd obviously planted flowers in a tribute to her dead son.

That was it. The canyon behind the school where Carlton had ended his life—that was where she'd taken Amanda.

He rushed back to the den and saw the brother slumped on the couch staring at the yearbook with all the pages that had been cut apart. A shoebox sat beside him on the couch, open. Justin gritted his teeth at the sight of the class rings inside the box.

"She did it," Ted mumbled in shock. "She kidnapped our classmates all these years...."

He looked lost as he stared up at Justin.

"Stay here and call me if she returns. I'm sending a crime scene team out here to pick up this stuff," Justin said.

Ted nodded, sagging on the couch with emotions. Justin felt sorry for him, but he had to save Amanda.

"I'm going to the canyon where Carlton jumped. I think your mother took Amanda there."

Pulse hammering, he ran to his SUV and raced from the drive, calling Lieutenant Gibbons on his way. He prayed he was right about the canyon as he sped down the road to the high school.

Seconds crawled, but it felt like an eternity until he reached the sign for Canyon High. He flipped off the lights and siren and parked in front of the school to avoid alerting Mrs. Butts of his arrival.

He eased the car door open and slid out, checking

his weapon as he scanned the area. He wondered if the security cameras had been fixed.

He crept around the side of the school to the back, searching for signs of Amanda and Mrs. Butts. Then he spotted it.

The door to the gate that separated the school property from the deepest part of the canyon. It stood open, making a grating sound as it swung back and forth in the wind.

His heart pounding, he moved along the bank of trees to the left, his weapon at the ready. Voices sounded to the right, and he inched closer.

Fear seized him when he saw Amanda on her knees with a gun to her forehead.

Breath tight in his chest, he took another step. Suddenly Mrs. Butts jerked Amanda up and dragged her closer to the edge of the canyon.

He couldn't wait. He had to make a move.

Vaulting into action, he crossed the next few feet, aiming for a clean shot at the woman. But suddenly Amanda lunged at Mrs. Butts, knocking her to the ground.

The gun fired, a grunt of pain echoing in the silence, and he ran forward, fear choking him. Was Amanda hit?

To the left, he spotted two other women he recognized from the yearbook as Julie and Lynn. They were struggling to free themselves.

The Butts woman had collapsed on top of Amanda. Was she hurt?

Amanda shoved the woman off of her with a grunt. Mrs. Butts lunged for her gun, but Justin raised his.

"It's over, Mrs. Butts," he said in a menacing tone. "Give it up or I'll shoot."

The woman stilled at the sound of his voice, then swung a sadistic look his way. "She has to die. It's not over till they're all punished."

"It is over," Amanda said calmly. "You've punished enough people. Carlton wouldn't want you to hurt Lynn or Julie or me."

"But you let him down!" she cried.

Justin inched closer. Julie and Lynn were sobbing and struggling with their bindings. Mrs. Butts slid her hands around Amanda's throat and tried to strangle her.

Justin was tempted to shoot. But Amanda was fighting the woman, and he was afraid he'd hit her. So he ran to them, grabbed the woman and dragged her off of Amanda.

She kicked and fought, but he was stronger, and he wrapped his arms around her waist, hauling her away. Amanda gasped for a breath, then pushed herself to her feet and ran to free the other women.

Justin threw Mrs. Butts down on the ground, rolled her to her stomach, jerked her arms behind her and slapped handcuffs around her wrists.

"Now it's over. And this time you're the one who's going to be punished."

WHEN AMANDA THOUGHT she might die, her life flashed in front of her. A life filled with police work, cases, murders and…living alone.

She suddenly yearned for more. A life with someone who loved her. With someone she loved.

Like Justin.

But that was crazy… He wasn't in love with her.

Sirens wailed as an ambulance arrived to examine Lynn and Julie. Except for shock, they appeared to be okay, but she had to play it by the book.

Her deputy arrived, along with Justin's supervisor, a crime team and another team that brought equipment to locate the bodies at the bottom of the canyon.

The next few hours were an ordeal as they began work to excavate the bodies. She left Justin to oversee the process while she drove Wynona Butts to the jail and locked her up.

"You can't do this," Wynona yelled. "They deserved to die."

"But not all the victims even attended our high school," Amanda said, mentally reviewing the list.

"No, but they knew Carlton, met him at different times. Middle school, church. They were all mean to him."

"You need help," Amanda said, her chest aching

for all the lost lives. "I'll see that you get it for Carlton's sake."

The woman continued to rant and scream as Amanda shut the door behind her. But Amanda tuned her out. At one time she'd felt sorry for her. But not after all the lives she'd taken and the pain she'd caused the victims' families.

Finally exhausted, Amanda slept on a cot in her office, determined to make sure Wynona didn't attempt suicide, and worried that when the victims' parents heard the news they'd bombard the jail and try to exact their own revenge.

By dawn, fatigue knotted her muscles, but she called a team to move Wynona to a more secure facility. By ten, she and Justin met for another press conference.

"We can now safely say that the missing women from our state have been found. Their families have been notified and will finally be able to put their loved ones to rest." A lump lodged in her throat, but she swallowed it back as she explained about Wynona Butts's arrest. "I suppose if there is a lesson in this it's that we, as parents and members of the town, should watch our teenagers more closely and teach them to be tolerant of others."

Hands flew up with questions, but she shook her head. "We're done here, folks. Justice will be served in a court of law."

And now maybe everyone in town could sleep soundly again.

THE REST OF the day Amanda and Justin spent meeting with family members of the missing women whose bodies had been recovered. Emotions ran high, relief to finally have answers mixing with anguish, shock and the sad realization that the missing women had been so close yet no one had guessed where they were.

Arrangements for autopsies were made, along with funerals, and a memorial service was held that evening at the church in town. A sunset vigil to mourn for the lives of the dead and the tragedies of the families who needed the town's support also was organized.

As Justin and Amanda left the service, a quiet descended between them.

The case was solved. It would take time for the residents to heal, but now that they knew the truth, they could begin the process.

He glanced at Amanda as they walked back to the jail. Maybe they could have one more night together, an evening to celebrate before he left Sunset Mesa.

His cell phone buzzed, and he checked the number. His chief. He punched Connect. "Sergeant Thorpe."

"Thorpe, listen, I know you just finished this case, and you did a fine job—"

"A lot of the credit goes to Sheriff Blair," he said, wanting to give Amanda her fair due.

"Sure, all right. I know you just finished, but we

just caught another case. If you want it, it's yours, but you'll need to go to Laredo right away."

Adrenaline surged through Justin. Another case on the heels of this one. He'd never turned down an opportunity to solve a crime.

Chasing bad guys was his life.

"I'll leave right away."

Amanda left the podium and walked toward him, and his heart did an odd flutter. A few minutes ago, all he could think about was getting her in bed again. Touching her. Loving her. Holding her another night. And maybe another...

Shaken by the thought, he squared his shoulders. "Good job, Amanda."

"You saved my life," she said. "Thank you for that."

He shrugged. "Just doing my job. Speaking of which," he said, his chest twitching with an odd pang, "I have to leave right now. Another case."

Something akin to disappointment flared in Amanda's eyes. Then again, maybe he'd imagined it, because a second later, she smiled, the professional, distant look she'd given him when they'd first met.

Before he'd seen her naked and touched and tasted every inch of her.

He wanted to do it again.

But she extended her hand for a handshake. "Thanks, Sergeant Thorpe. It's been a pleasure working with you. Good luck."

His gaze met hers, and a moment of tension rippled between them. His chest squeezed, the urge to say something more nagging at him.

He felt as if he was leaving something important behind.

But she shook his hand, then turned and walked toward her car, and he felt like a fool. She obviously didn't have feelings for him.

She was independent, smart…and beautiful. And married to her job just as he was.

*The perfect woman for you.*

And if he didn't snap her up, someone else would.

That would be for the best, he reminded himself as he climbed in his SUV and headed out of town.

He didn't do emotions. And he didn't have room or time for anything else in his life.

## Chapter Twenty-Four

Amanda bit her lip to keep her emotions at bay as she watched Justin drive away. She was a big girl. A strong, independent woman.

She did not need a man.

She'd always known that her time with Justin was limited. Work related. Nothing more.

So why was she crying?

Because Justin was the first man she'd met who understood her drive to do her job, understood her need to solve crimes.

And respected her for her work.

He'd also made her body sing with erotic sensations that she'd never experienced before.

But that wasn't all. She had fallen in love with him.

Stupid, stupid, stupid.

Falling for any man was crazy in her line of work, much less for a Texas Ranger who might leave one morning to go to work and end up in a body bag that night.

So could she.

She swiped at her tears as she parked at her house, let herself in and jumped in the shower. The memory of looking down at that canyon and imagining herself at the bottom taunted her.

Yes, she could have died last night. And if she had, would anyone have cared?

Would she spend the rest of her life alone because she was too afraid of losing someone to actually allow love in her life?

JUSTIN STOPPED AT the crossroads leading out of town, the moonlight dappling a golden glow across the horizon. If he drove all night he could make it to Laredo by morning. Find a hotel, grab a shower and hot breakfast and be working the case before noon.

The canyon to the left caught his eye, its vastness stretching far and wide, from behind the high school to the edge of town. A hollow emptiness resounded from the canyon tonight as if the ghosts had finally been raised and the dead could rest.

Amanda had almost died there. If he'd been a few minutes later, they might be dragging her broken body from the bottom.

His stomach seized into a knot.

He'd never been so afraid in his life.

Because he loved her.

He punched the steering wheel with his fist and spun the SUV around. He didn't want to drive all night to a new crime scene. The chief had other agents who could do the job.

He wanted the night off. Wanted to hold Amanda in his arms and make love to her again and whisper sweet nothings to her while he could.

His heart throbbed as he raced to her place, and when he arrived and saw a dim light glowing in the bedroom, adrenaline surged through him. He jumped from the SUV and hurried up to the door. He had no idea what he'd say, but he couldn't leave Sunset Mesa tonight.

He couldn't leave Amanda.

He pounded on the door, perspiration trickling down the back of his neck. A second later, she opened the door. Her eyes looked red rimmed as if she might have been crying, and he wondered if something else bad had happened.

He inhaled a breath, but the scent of some feminine body wash wafted from her, and he realized she'd just come from the shower. Her gorgeous hair lay in damp tendrils around her shoulders, a bead of water lingering at the top of her breasts where her satin robe had parted.

"What's wrong?" she asked. "I thought you had to leave."

"You've been crying," he said in a hoarse whisper. "Why?"

Her eyes misted over, and she squeezed them shut as if to stem more tears. Fear clogged his throat and he gripped her arms. "What happened?"

Her gaze met his, other emotions filling the depths. Hunger, passion, need.

"I missed you," she said, her cheeks stained with a blush. "Why did you come back?"

"For you," he said, emboldened by the fact that she'd actually cried over him. It was foolish, but it gave him hope. "I...don't want to go to Laredo tonight."

"I don't want you to go either," she said softly.

"I want you." He lowered his head and kissed her. "Tonight. Tomorrow. Always."

She slid her arms around him and kissed him back. "What are you saying, Justin?"

"That I love you," he murmured against her ear. "I almost lost you last night and that scared me."

"We could both die on the job."

"We could." He teased her neck with his lips. "So we might as well enjoy what we have together."

"I love you, too," she said, a seductive smile lighting her eyes. "Come on in, cowboy."

He chuckled and let her lead him to the bedroom. Seconds later, they lay naked in each other's arms, words of love spilling out as they joined their bodies again and again through the night.

\* \* \* \* \*

# LARGER-PRINT BOOKS!
## GET 2 FREE LARGER-PRINT NOVELS PLUS
## 2 FREE GIFTS!

**HARLEQUIN®**

# INTRIGUE®

### BREATHTAKING ROMANTIC SUSPENSE

**YES!** Please send me 2 FREE LARGER-PRINT Harlequin Intrigue® novels and my 2 FREE gifts (gifts are worth about $10). After receiving them, if I don't wish to receive any more books, I can return the shipping statement marked "cancel." If I don't cancel, I will receive 6 brand-new novels every month and be billed just $5.49 per book in the U.S. or $5.99 per book in Canada. That's a saving of at least 13% off the cover price! It's quite a bargain! Shipping and handling is just 50¢ per book in the U.S. and 75¢ per book in Canada.* I understand that accepting the 2 free books and gifts places me under no obligation to buy anything. I can always return a shipment and cancel at any time. Even if I never buy another book, the two free books and gifts are mine to keep forever.

199/399 HDN F42Y

Name _____ (PLEASE PRINT)

Address _____ Apt. #

City _____ State/Prov. _____ Zip/Postal Code

Signature (if under 18, a parent or guardian must sign)

#### Mail to the **Harlequin® Reader Service:**
**IN U.S.A.:** P.O. Box 1867, Buffalo, NY 14240-1867
**IN CANADA:** P.O. Box 609, Fort Erie, Ontario L2A 5X3

**Are you a subscriber to Harlequin Intrigue books
and want to receive the larger-print edition?
Call 1-800-873-8635 today or visit www.ReaderService.com.**

\* Terms and prices subject to change without notice. Prices do not include applicable taxes. Sales tax applicable in N.Y. Canadian residents will be charged applicable taxes. Offer not valid in Quebec. This offer is limited to one order per household. Not valid for current subscribers to Harlequin Intrigue Larger-Print books. All orders subject to credit approval. Credit or debit balances in a customer's account(s) may be offset by any other outstanding balance owed by or to the customer. Please allow 4 to 6 weeks for delivery. Offer available while quantities last.

**Your Privacy**—The Harlequin® Reader Service is committed to protecting your privacy. Our Privacy Policy is available online at www.ReaderService.com or upon request from the Harlequin Reader Service.

We make a portion of our mailing list available to reputable third parties that offer products we believe may interest you. If you prefer that we not exchange your name with third parties, or if you wish to clarify or modify your communication preferences, please visit us at www.ReaderService.com/consumerschoice or write to us at Harlequin Reader Service Preference Service, P.O. Box 9062, Buffalo, NY 14269. Include your complete name and address.

HILP13R

# REQUEST YOUR FREE BOOKS!
## 2 FREE RIVETING INSPIRATIONAL NOVELS
## PLUS 2 FREE MYSTERY GIFTS

*Love Inspired*®
# SUSPENSE

**YES!** Please send me 2 FREE Love Inspired® Suspense novels and my 2 FREE mystery gifts (gifts are worth about $10). After receiving them, if I don't wish to receive any more books, I can return the shipping statement marked "cancel." If I don't cancel, I will receive 4 brand-new novels every month and be billed just $4.74 per book in the U.S. or $5.24 per book in Canada. That's a savings of at least 21% off the cover price. It's quite a bargain! Shipping and handling is just 50¢ per book in the U.S. and 75¢ per book in Canada.* I understand that accepting the 2 free books and gifts places me under no obligation to buy anything. I can always return a shipment and cancel at any time. Even if I never buy another book, the two free books and gifts are mine to keep forever.

123/323 IDN F5AN

| | |
|---|---|
| Name | (PLEASE PRINT) |
| Address | Apt. # |
| City | State/Prov. | Zip/Postal Code |

Signature (if under 18, a parent or guardian must sign)

### Mail to the **Harlequin**® **Reader Service:**
**IN U.S.A.:** P.O. Box 1867, Buffalo, NY 14240-1867
**IN CANADA:** P.O. Box 609, Fort Erie, Ontario L2A 5X3

**Are you a current subscriber to Love Inspired Suspense books and want to receive the larger-print edition?**
**Call 1-800-873-8635 or visit www.ReaderService.com.**

\* Terms and prices subject to change without notice. Prices do not include applicable taxes. Sales tax applicable in N.Y. Canadian residents will be charged applicable taxes. Offer not valid in Quebec. This offer is limited to one order per household. Not valid for current subscribers to Love Inspired Suspense books. All orders subject to credit approval. Credit or debit balances in a customer's account(s) may be offset by any other outstanding balance owed by or to the customer. Please allow 4 to 6 weeks for delivery. Offer available while quantities last.

**Your Privacy**—The Harlequin® Reader Service is committed to protecting your privacy. Our Privacy Policy is available online at www.ReaderService.com or upon request from the Harlequin Reader Service.
We make a portion of our mailing list available to reputable third parties that offer products we believe may interest you. If you prefer that we not exchange your name with third parties, or if you wish to clarify or modify your communication preferences, please visit us at www.ReaderService.com/consumerschoice or write to us at Harlequin Reader Service Preference Service, P.O. Box 9062, Buffalo, NY 14269. Include your complete name and address.

LISDIR13R

# *ReaderService*.com

## Manage your account online!

- Review your order history
- Manage your payments
- Update your address

*We've designed
the Harlequin® Reader Service
website just for you.*

## Enjoy all the features!

- Reader excerpts from any series
- Respond to mailings and
  special monthly offers
- Discover new series available to you
- Browse the Bonus Bucks catalog
- Share your feedback

*Visit us at:*
## ReaderService.com